Sincerely, Mother

Boma Somiari

Contents

1

Mum Brain, Hormones, and All That

All I'd wanted was just a quiet Sunday at church — to sing a hymn or two, say a prayer, and hear something from the sermon. Apparently, it was too much to ask for.

It began when the children decided they'd had enough of church, just mere minutes after we arrived.

"I'm hungry. Can we go now?" my son begged.

"We can go after church".

"When?"

"After they finish preaching and praying", I handed him a programme and pen, "Shh, write letters A to Z and numbers 1 to 10", I told him.

Then his sister realised her bow had come undone — and she doesn't like undone bows — they almost give her a panic attack, I think, because she begged for the bow to be fixed like her life depended on it. And she didn't bother to do so quietly because… well, her life depended on it.

After my son stopped writing at letter C, wanting to go and pee, I turned to their father for help.

He was lifting up holy hands and worshipping the one true God.

Maybe I was exhausted. Maybe I just needed a little help....

Because usually, I don't really mind tending the children, but on this particular day I didn't think it was fair that he could worship in peace while the children were getting biscuit in my hair, and crying when I said they couldn't be dogs when they grow up. And then there was the frosty looks I was getting from fellow worshippers.

Plus, it absolutely didn't help that he still looked spruce and tidy when all he had to do this morning was pick a suit and a pair of shoes, and brush his teeth, while I spent all that time in front of the mirror and now look like I've just finished mowing the lawn. Or maybe like I've just emerged from the kitchen after another cooking fail.

I didn't think it was fair, and I told him so.

"Are you pregnant?"

"What?'

"You're acting weird".

We were in church so I tried to behave.

When I told him his son needed to pee, he looked relieved to go with him.

As another congregational hymn began, I tried to sing with them but they were back after only three lines, and now my daughter wanted her hand cut off.

Again, she believed her life depended on it, so she wasn't asking quietly.

"Cut it off! Cut it off!" she wailed "He sneezed on it".

"Shh", there were those frosty looks again, as I tried to placate her (and I did my best to deflect the looks). "Cut what off?"

"My hand".

Dear Lord. She held out her right hand like it really needed to be cut off.

"Why?"

She elbowed her brother and regarded him like he was the bane of her existence "Because he sneezed on it".

OK. Makes perfect sense.

"Ok, we'll cut it off when we get home".

"When?"

"After they finish preaching and praying".

"OK".

I must have looked pitiable (I still had the lawnmower and ambitious cook look thing going for me). Or maybe she was an angel sent from heaven just for me. Or maybe she just understood….

But as I lifted my head after having this perfectly logical conversation with my daughter, my eyes fell on an older woman. She nodded and smiled, and suddenly it wasn't all that bad that I couldn't have a quiet Sunday at church. Or sing a hymn or two, say a prayer, and hear something from the sermon. It wasn't all that bad that after all that time spent in front of the mirror, I now look like I've just finished mowing the lawn. Or like I've just emerged from the kitchen after another cooking fail (plus, I no longer held it all that much against Spruce and Tidy that all he had to do this morning was pick a suit and a pair of shoes, and brush his teeth).

I smiled back and mouthed my thanks.

And then I held the smile for the rest of the service, thoroughly getting under the skin of prim and proper fellow worshippers, and terrifying Spruce and Tidy, so much so that I had to explain about off mum days, wanting to run away. And, well…

Hormones.

Now he was convinced we were expecting.

****

I read a blog one time where they explained mum brain and why it's not that strange that I keep forgetting things — I lose my train of thought easily, walk into a room and forget why I'm there, and look for my phone while I'm using it….

It's hard to traverse this path I'm on now, and sometimes I think life dealt me this hand so that it can be entertained, watching me make a futile attempt at being successful with it (OK, I'll admit this line of thought comes after I've been awake for three whole days. It comes with the mum brain, apparently).

It must be the reason we went to the store to get ice cream after church, and we left without ice cream because I forgot to buy it.

We had this fundraiser at church and someone thought it was a good idea to sell ice cream after the service let out. Maybe it was a good idea, but they were asking for more than a day's wage. And I thought it bordered on extortion.

Spruce and Tidy said that was the whole point since they were trying to raise money. I said we can buy ice cream at the store on our way home.

Since the children were nearing the meltdown point (as it seemed like everyone else was getting ice cream) and I wasn't about to be cajoled, we reached the consensus that we'd stop by the store on our way home (I may or may not have threatened to go on vacation if my stance wasn't adopted).

And then I forgot to buy it.

It's easy to see how it could have happened this time, though.

So, what happened was….

Spruce and Tidy had been on the phone for what seemed like forever after we reached the store. I thought I'd save time by going in to get the ice cream instead of waiting endlessly for him. My daughter wanted to go with me. At least it was just her. Her brother had found something that held his attention, and I didn't think there would be any problems going with her.

We were fine until my sister called to ask about a family recipe. Was she supposed to add in the eggs first or the butter? I told my mum to write a family recipe cookbook. She said if we'd join her in the kitchen she wouldn't need to write one. She should have just written that book....

Because then my sister wouldn't have called, and I wouldn't have been distracted and taken my eyes off my daughter who in that sparse time had managed to send an entire row of merchandise crashing to the ground.

If I wasn't too embarrassed, and trying to ascertain how much our budget for the month had been upended, I would have been impressed. *I mean, how did she do that?*

Thankfully, nothing was damaged. But the manager was not pleased. If the frosty looks at church were cold, the glare of fellow shoppers was chilling. I even heard a comment about incapable mothers raising entitled children.

I picked up my daughter and made for the door. I couldn't get out fast enough.

Spruce and Tidy was still on the phone, but I begged him to drive, "We need to leave now. Please go! Go!"

I tried, but I couldn't answer very coherently, all the questions he asked on the drive home.

"Where's the ice cream?'

"Ice cream?" I was thoroughly confused for a while and had absolutely no idea what he was talking about.

And I must have been a pitiable sight to behold. Either that, or I may have looked ready to explode with something, because Spruce and Tidy began the drive home.

And it was a long, quiet drive…. (OK, I'm not quite sure. I might have heard chattering coming from the back, and chidings from the driver's seat… but I'm not sure….)

But next thing I know, we're home and everybody's waiting on me for food — because they're hungry — imagine that!

I mentioned that we all just got back home together, and I'm hungry too.

While they ate, I made a brief stop at my forte (OK, it's my wardrobe) and dug out the box of chocolate I'd snuck in there the last time I needed to make a getaway. It was just the last piece remaining, and even that they wouldn't let me eat in peace.

I hurriedly ate the sweet as I heard footsteps approaching. But they were faster than I'd anticipated.

Opening the wardrobe, my daughter asked what I was eating.

When my son began to search the area for *only-heaven-knows-what*, I felt like a suspect caught with exhibits in an ongoing investigation.

Because here I was, in my wardrobe, with a half-eaten sweet in my hand, trying to swallow what was already in my mouth.

This was pathetic! I froze for a bit as the realisation hit me—

I'm a grown woman and these children cannot be doing this to me (And also, my mama used to say, "Do what you need to do. You can't fill others out of an empty well". So it's not like I was doing anything wrong).

"What are you looking for?" I asked my son.

"Where did you hide the sweets?"

My daughter began to cry, "I need to pee".

And just like that, the conundrum of how they find me — Every. Blessed. Time! — began to assault my mind.

Your father can get you all the sweets you want and help you pee. Why won't you just ask him?

And how did you even find me?

It's like they can smell you out wherever you are, and they will find you if you breathe.

They'd walk right past their father and come all the way to the kitchen to ask you to open a pack of snacks.

And when they start to argue? Sometimes I feel like I might blow up (like, pray, who cares who finished breakfast first? And why do you have to be so loud?)

I know, these are not very motherly thoughts to think, but still….

Do not cry. Do not cry. And do not try to lie and say you're not their real mother. I admonished myself and did my best to heed that counsel, but when I remembered that they invaded my forte while leaving Spruce and Tidy to his own devices, something came undone.

Let's just blame it on mum brain.

****

We've been told that seasons don't last forever.

And this season of motherhood won't last forever. We're supposed to hold on to it as long as we can.

Maybe that's how you deal with these kinds of days.

That might be, but all I'd wanted was just a quiet Sunday at church — to sing a hymn or two, say a prayer, and hear something from the sermon….

Sometimes all you need is a little help. Like when Spruce and Tidy came and got the kids so I could be left alone for a while (let's just ignore the fact that the house was dripping with Ice Cream and candy wraps by the time I was ready to come out of my forte).

14

When you really think about it though, all we can give is all that's required of us.

I may not always have it all under control, but as long as we're still here, we'd keep going, doing the best we can, and believing that it would all come together in the end.

Because children, truly, are a gift from the Lord. I really believe that (on some days, at least).

2

Do Not Teach Her Children Those Things

"There's an app for everything, these days".

I tried to behave, and not lose my head as my friend talked my ears off, trying to get me as excited about the subject as she was. And she just went on and on and on….

"Did you know there's an app that helps you track how long you've been on your phone?"

"No, I didn't know that".

"There's one that helps you count calories".

"I didn't know that".

"And another one that's like your very own personal assistant".

"Really?" I tried to tone down the sarcasm, but I couldn't help it as a significant amount still found its way to my voice and the smile that followed, "Is there one that helps you watch your kids while you stalk and troll on Facebook and Twitter?"

Now she started to go around like a bear with a sorehead.

I only wanted to help.

I was there to help her watch the kids because she was sick, and she also had a deadline to beat.

I'd told her I had to do housecleaning on my blog — begged her even. I even suggested she called her mother, but she said her mother would not believe her. And then she had tried to blackmail me with a speech about how friends are supposed to have each other's back and help pull each other up, and how it is the Christian thing to do, "Even the Bible says a friend is supposed to stick closer than a brother."

There are at least two things wrong with that reference to Scripture you just tried to make. Number one, I'm not your brother. Number two, I don't think that's what it says, and it doesn't even apply here....

"All you'd have to do is feed them and put them in front of the TV", she begged.

Nothing was said about this earful I was now a recipient of, about her recent discovery of the wonderful world of apps.

The understanding had been that I would watch the kids and cover as much ground as I could with my blog, while she tried to recover from her illness and beat her deadline.

But the moment she let me in, she grabbed her phone and went into a tirade about how social media enables destructive behaviours and tendencies, like when people portray falsities and act like they believe the lies they're telling.

She was on Facebook.

Then she went on about how people fall for the lure of self-importance because they have a few thousand followers on social media, "Did you know you can buy followers? In blocks, as in, in thousands, and at very cheap rates."

She was on Twitter.

When she began to talk about how people think it's OK to hide behind a keyboard and leave comments laced with fury and vitriol on the internet, I asked her if she was feeling better already.

She said she had a headache and no energy at all. And the thought came to my mind that it wasn't for no reason, if her mother didn't believe her.

I told her she didn't have to use the internet if it got her all worked up, but she said we were no longer in the eighteenth century. Then, as if I didn't already know it, she informed me she was a writer.

And then she made the outrageous assertion that writing goes hand in hand with the use of the internet.

Please! Almost every writer knows that excuse and more than a few have used that classic at least one time.

More hours passed, and she was still with the phone, discovering more of what was wrong with the internet.

This time it was falsities propounded by brethren from Church — brothers and sisters that were supposed to be witnesses of the truth, standing for, and by it in this lost world.

"Judgment truly would begin in the house of God", she said, as I tried to get her two-year-old to see that it was better to eat from a plate instead of the floor, "That's in the Bible, right?"

I was busy, so I ignored the question (Ok, I ignored her).

When I didn't respond, she tried again, "There's this app in my phone I can make memes with, and I want to make one with that Scripture so people would stop lying".

I've been told that I don't need to try to be sarcastic because I was born that way, so when I feigned interest and pretended to share her enthusiasm, I wasn't trying to be sarcastic or anything like that, I was just being true to my own self.

"Isn't there an app to find Scripture references with?"

"You can do almost everything with apps these days", she said, "I could find one! Thank you!"

When she began to gush over the notion of how two good heads are better than one, I did my best to not scoff and roll my eyes, but they might have glazed over just a little bit.

You know how they say if you can't find your children, and your house is unusually quiet, then you might have a situation on your hands? Best believe mama knows what she's talking about when she tells you so.

I've found that to be true on many occasions so when the house became unusually quiet, I went from room to room looking for the kids I was supposed to be watching, praying the whole time that we wouldn't be putting out a fire, rushing a child to the hospital to flush out poison from his system, or figuring out how soon insurance can be claimed on some property.

OK, I know my imagination can run away like that sometimes, but I'm a writer, so… there's that. But imagine my shock when I walked in the bathroom and saw my friend's five-year-old watching a video on her phone that showed how to cut your wrist.

OK, so let's stay focused and not be distracted by the question of why a child that young had her own phone. That's a question for another day.

The question that begged an answer now was, had I really seen what I thought I'd seen, or was it just the imagination thing happening again?

I took the phone from her and started to watch the video from the beginning. It didn't take that long to realise that this was fire that needed to be put out. It was an animated video that could have been missed had it not been for mama's counsel to keep a watchful eye on children. It told the story of a boy who had suffered constant bullying at school and decided he'd had enough. He was going to cut his wrist but didn't cut far enough so he ended up in the hospital instead. It then went on to show what he did wrong, and how he could have done it instead.

By the end of the video, I wondered just how big this fire was, because there were other videos with disturbing content being pushed with big, flashing red call-to-action buttons. There was one about boys who were actually girls, and girls who were born as boys. There was also the one about hearing voices in your head, and people talking to you that only you could see. And the one about how having two mummies or two daddies is still the same as having a mummy and a daddy. And another one teaching new words for boys who were born as girls, and girls who were born as boys.

I must have said out loud, some things I'd intended to only think because by then she was already shaking, thoroughly frightened, and begging me not to tell her mother.

"How long have you been watching these videos?" I asked her.

"I don't know", she said, "I just watch whatever comes up".

"So you've seen a lot of these". It was both a statement and a question, but more a statement that conveyed my assessment of the situation.

My tone must have reflected it because she became hysterical and frantic in her pleadings for me to not tell her mother.

And then her mother walked in, "Please don't tell me what?"

✳✳✳✳

It took a while before we could calm the crying child down enough to help her understand that she wasn't to be blamed for the situation at hand. At least not entirely.

Apart from a few bookmarked sites her mother deemed safe for children, she wasn't allowed to use the internet. And then there were also the game apps. It was while she had been using one of those apps that she had watched the video.

"It's supposed to be for children", her mother fumed. She showed me the app again, as if she hadn't already done so mere minutes before, and as if I didn't already know it was an app popular with children.

I might not be that taken by the world of apps, but I don't live in a cave. I meant to tell her that but decided against it almost immediately. She was already furious, and pointing this small fact out might have proved combustible, adding to the already raging conflagration. And, it didn't help that I had no understanding of how this whole situation might have happened.

"It's an app for children, for crying out loud!" She showed me the app again. "Why would they teach children how to kill themselves? And the videos are animated so without looking, we'd think they're telling them to eat their vegetables and be kind to strangers."

"Maybe there's a backdoor some people took advantage of", I reminded her.

"It's not an app you need the internet for", she said, throwing her hands up, "And I went through the security settings and did everything right. The videos were already probably there. They came, shipped with the game! These people were purposeful with this wickedness!"

We don't really know how these things work. But let's not bring that up, because she was now not only like a bear with a sore head, she was also madder than a wet hen.

"Do you see what I did?"

I had no idea what she was talking about, and for some reason, I didn't think it would be wise to answer too quickly. So I bided my time and pretended to give watch to the two-year-old who had just woken up from a nap. He was having none of it, but I just held the cup to his mouth, praying his mama explains her point fast before he gets tired and leaves.

"I helped these people teach my daughter these things".

Are you serious right now? That was unexpected, and not very easy to respond to.

But when you looked at it again, she wasn't all that off the mark. So what do you say to a friend in this situation?

The two-year-old chose that moment to dip his hand in the cup, tipping it and pouring the whole content on the rug.

Bad timing, child! She looked ready to pounce on him, so I snatched him while she was still considering the notion and handed him to his sister. Any other day, she would have kicked him out and locked the door — literally — but not today. Today, this five-year-old was a child willing to do anything to make whatever wrong she thought she had done, go away.

She was such a sorry sight, as was her mother.

This was absolutely nothing like I had envisioned the day going when I'd agreed to help my friend watch her kids. So far, my blog had been completely abandoned, while I acted as chief security detail and personal assistant to two very active children. It was nothing like just feeding them and putting them in front of the TV at all.

And now, their mother was coming apart at the seams. I mean, she was pacing, talking to herself, and plotting a complete takedown of the world of apps.

"I need you to help me research the world of apps and how they're stealing our children from us", she told me.

It was like the kind of thought that hits you like a thunderbolt and leaves you trying to regain your balance.

Usually, when she gets these ideas, you just can never know where the train of thoughts leads everyone on board with her. And I wasn't exactly feeling up to that kind of ride.

I was thinking, *we need to calm down and tread this path that's calling us now really carefully,* but you know that thing that happens when you imagine something a certain way, and it comes out nothing like how you imagined it (and not in a good way)?

Well, it happened again, because my thinking chose to come out in just one word, "Why?"

She looked stunned, "Why?" She said, "How can you even ask me that? You were the one who found her in the bathroom".

"I don't know what you have in mind, but you can't just take down the entire world of apps by yourself. You don't even know anything about it", I reminded her.

"That's why we're going to find out all we can".

We? I thought it best to keep my mouth shut because she wouldn't have liked my thinking on that subject of we, as in, she and I.

I was as angry as she was, but my stance was still the same — we needed to tread this path carefully.

"At least wait till your husband returns", I told her, trying to delay whatever irrational move she was already plotting.

"Two weeks is too long to wait".

"But you'd have had time to consider your options by then".

"We need to start immediately, now that the fire's still burning".

There was that *we* again.

When I told her our priority at the moment should be checking on her daughter, she said something about stoking the flames while you still had fuel. And then she went straight to her computer.

For a moment, I almost felt sorry for those who would be on the receiving end of this angst. Her gait was an outright war cry. I had no idea what she had in mind, but she wasn't playing.

As I went to check on her children, she called out, "Nothing is insignificant. We need all the information we can lay our hands on".

"There's no *we* on this journey you're embarking on", I muttered, trying hard to not spew the thinking on my mind.

****

Two weeks later, after countless emails back and forth, endless phone calls (even at night) and tons of coffee to help match her drive, she put out an article that went viral in less than a day.

In only a few hours, hashtags were trending, the article was picked up by major blogs and news outlets, and mothers were sharing their experiences. There were calls for boycotts. And some leading app creators even put out statements and disclaimers.

It was bigger than we could have ever imagined (OK, maybe just me) but she worked on this project like her life depended on it, and with a drive that was not that easy to keep up with.

No, she did not take down the world of apps, but she did get her message across.

When she began to receive emails threatening litigations, I wondered if we had gone too far, but she said we had nothing to be afraid of, since we only told the truth.

We? OK, I know I helped with the article and with promoting it on social media, but I'd thought we were passed the *we* stage already.

It wasn't a challenge that lasted long though because almost immediately, there were lawyers lining up, offering their services free of charge.

I said it was a miracle, the impact her article had made. It was like it started a movement. All she had done was share her story (well, that, and all the ways we could find that exposed people to content deliberately set to corrupt minds. And there are many), but she said there's power in sharing our stories and telling the truth. And we shortchange ourselves when we underestimate the opportunity social media affords us to make an impact with the truth, for good.

She does have a point.

And mama was always right —

Please find your children if you don't know where they are, and the house is unusually quiet.

But the biggest takeaway from all of this would be to never cross a mama on a day when she's about her business like a bear with a sorehead and madder than a wet hen.

Do not teach her children new words like zie and tey.

And definitely, do not teach them how to cut their wrists.

3

Finding Roses in This Bed of Thorns

I did not try to burn down my house with my children in it.

Sometimes I forget it's my story they're trying to tell when I hear of the woman who planned to kill her children. I shudder to think that a mother would pour fuel on her children, light them up, and then watch them burn.

That woman is not me.

I am a mother trying to keep her children from their father, and also keep them alive long enough for me to be able to say "I did it".

****

They say life is not a bed of roses. Sometimes I think it is a bed of thorns. For some of us, at least.

And the thorns flourished.

I desperately sought a place of oblivion, a place where I could forget my reality and create worlds that were kind to me. I'd given my honest best in this bed of thorns, after all. I'd paid my dues, and I have my scars to show for it.

Alcohol took me to that place, but before long I realised that the solace it provided was a lie. Its ultimate purpose was to finally do me in.

This realisation didn't help my cause though because I still wanted that place of oblivion.

With two children, failing hope, and a man that took his frustrations out on me, it just kept getting worse.

It's not like there were no jobs, I just couldn't keep one long enough because of that ultimate purpose to undo me.

There have been days when I let my children go hungry because I'd spent the last money on me on a drink. Then I'd scream at them and beat them when they wouldn't stop crying because they were hungry.

I can't even remember all the times total strangers have shown up at my door with my children, because in my drunken state, I'd forgotten to pick them up from school.

And then there was that day when I'd just lost a job again. I'd gotten home to find my children at home. *What happened?* At least I'd remembered to take them to school.

"What happened?" I'd screamed at my five-year-old son.

"There's no school today. It's Saturday".

"I told you we should have stayed in school", his younger sister whispered, and then she started to cry.

Maybe she was afraid they'd get beaten again. Maybe she was afraid they'd have to clean the house after I'd messed it up again. For whatever reason, she wouldn't stop crying.

And the fact just grated on my nerves.

I dragged them, kicking and screaming, and locked them in a room, "to think about what you've done", I told them.

I had no idea what they had done, but in my drunken state, it had seemed like a terrible thing.

I don't remember what happened in the space of time after I'd locked them up, and before the bucket of water was poured on me.

It took a while before I could figure out what was going on.

Two doors had been broken to get into the house, and to my children.

My children.

The house was filled with smoke, and neighbours were trying to put out the fire.

I'd tried to cook before I'd fallen asleep. The house was a mess, and too many things lay around to carry the fire.

"Where are my children, please?"

Nobody was talking to me.

✳✳✳✳

It was the beginning of a time of awakening. Slowly, but surely, hope began to come alive again. Maybe if I looked more closely, I might find some roses in this bed of thorns.

It took a bit of effort, but I started to look.

After I found my closest friend lying in a pool of her own blood, unconscious, some of my priorities were rearranged.

I'd travelled home for the first time in over a decade to surprise her for her birthday, but I'd ended up staying at the hospital with her for two weeks, watching her fight for her life, trying to recover from injuries suffered at the hands of the father of her children.

It was in that hospital room that I promised myself and my comatose friend that I would think hard about my priorities and forge a new path that would lead to a state of existence without my children's father. It shouldn't be that hard to follow that path. I only have to remember the countless times I've hurriedly wiped my own blood from various walls and floors in the house to keep the children from seeing it. At other times I've had the difficult task of trying to make my stories match as I explained bruises and swellings. I tried everything — *I fell in the pool. I cut myself while making dinner. I missed my steps and tumbled down the stairs.*

I even tried the *I-don't-know-how-that-happened* story. "It wasn't there yesterday", I would say. Usually, my hearers would look at me with sympathy and offer what I suppose was meant to be advice, but sounded to me like they were saying "We don't believe you".

Finally, I stopped trying and would lock myself in the house for days. Until I discovered how much makeup could hide.

A plan began to form in my mind. I would go back, get my kids and some money, and begin to forge that new path — immediately after my friend is discharged from the hospital.

It wasn't a very difficult decision to make because unlike my friend, I wasn't married to the father of my children.

While we waited for her to wake up, I wrote down goals and strategies. The longer we waited, the more I elaborated on the plan — I would do whatever work I could find to support myself while I go back to school and try to raise two children as a single mother. Eventually, I would qualify as a lawyer and go after every person I could find like this man who convinced me to leave home as a teenager. He'd said we could claim the world if we worked hard enough. And then I woke up one morning and realised I was stuck with a friend bent on sucking life from me. Every. Single. Day.

✳✳✳✳

I remember that morning very well.

I'd woken up with a start, and a definite sense of looming danger. Even my unconscious friend looked agitated, but I thought I was imagining things.

I looked around the hospital room that had become home for about two weeks, trying to see if there was anything unusual or out of place. Nothing stood out. I read a few verses from the Scriptures, and some of the devotional blogs I subscribed to. It felt rushed.

I tried to pray but was too restless to get enough meaningful sentences out.

Usually, worship music helped to calm me — unless I was in a state of acute fear and distress — then, only Jesus could.

It was one of those days.

I'd delayed getting breakfast until sometime around noon when it became somewhat difficult to deal with the protestations of my stomach — OK, I'd admit it just this one time — I was almost at the point of starting to see stars from hunger. Even then, I stalled for as much as I could because of the sense of foreboding that had been quickly claiming space in my mind. But the protestations were severe! Finally, I decided I'd get something from the food vendors and hurry back to the room, instead of waiting endlessly in line for one of the finer alternatives offered by the restaurant on the premises.

I was barely out of the lobby when without thinking, I turned around, almost running back to the room.

There was a man in the room — which was strange — because no one knew where we were. I'd made sure of that. And we'd had no visitors in the two weeks we had been there.

All those weeks of her calling to talk about how she needed to get away with the children, and then finding her in a pool of her own blood... I didn't bother to call her husband. The last time her husband travelled, she'd sent the children as far away as she could, to a friend — because every time she sent them to her parents, he went and got them back. And she needed them as far away from him as she could get them, while she plotted her escape.

For years, I told her, just get up and go. She said she would if her parents weren't elders at church, and if the church wouldn't frown so much on that course of action.

I told her she might as well pick a date and start planning her funeral. She said I should remove the log in my eyes first, so I'd see clearly to remove the speck in hers.

Her meaning was completely lost on me until that moment my priorities were rearranged.

So no, we weren't expecting any visitors in that hospital room. And it was a problem that there was a man in the room, more so, as I didn't recognise him.

Standing in the doorway, I bit my tongue, trying to keep from spewing the vitriol threatening to spill — I was hungry, tired, and not ready to deal with whatever drama was about to unfold. Add to that, the amplification of the sense of looming danger, it was the perfect mix for complete perplexity and disorientation.

In my hurry to get food and be back as soon as I could, I had left my phone in the room. No one else was in sight — nurses, doctors, people visiting other patients — no one. I was not about to take my eyes off this man that looked like he could uproot a tree with bare hands.

"Are you lost, sir?" I heard myself say, as I tried to both look around and not take my eyes off him.

"I heard what happened, and I had to come".

Save us, dear Lord! Since he didn't hear it from me, he had to have heard it from the man by whose hands she was lying unconscious on that bed.

Except someone else had witnessed what happened.

When I said nothing and just continued staring, he started to empty the contents of the bags he'd been holding on the table.

I might not have been sure of a lot of things about life at that time, but I did know this —

I don't know this man. I don't know how or why he's here, and I'm not eating his food.

So I told him.

"We don't need food", I blurted out, before I had time to think about it and change my mind.

That shocked him — well, at least he looked shocked when he raised his head.

I was still in the doorway, wondering why no one else was passing by at this time, and praying that someone would. I don't know this man. He's giving me both food and serious cause for concern at the same time.

Probably finally sensing my unease, he stretched out his hand, "My name is —"

Thank You, Lord! Finally!

I have never been happier seeing a doctor in my whole, entire life!

And the haste with which this strange man left upon seeing the doctor substantiated the unrest I'd been feeling the whole time.

As he hurried to leave, I reminded him about the food he'd brought — even when I'm starving, I still remember all mama told me about stranger-danger — especially when the stranger thoroughly terrifies you.

After he left, I mentioned my concerns to the doctor. He said he had stopped by because he noticed how troubled I looked.

Arrangements were made to see that we didn't receive any more visitors.

But I still couldn't shake off that sense of foreboding. And I needed to find out who that man was, and what his purpose was.

****

Sleep didn't come easy that night.

After convincing myself that it was best to keep my family out of the situation, in a moment of uncertainty, I'd sent my mother a text explaining the situation.

She replied with a torrent of messages.

"I'm at Bible study. I'd call you when I get home".

"Ok", I replied.

And then —

"Make sure the doors and windows are locked before you sleep". "Have you eaten?" "Where are the children now?" "Do you have your Bible with you? Read it and pray the Scriptures over what's happening now". "Are you learning from what has happened to your friend? "Are you getting my messages? I don't know what's wrong with this phone".

I'm not replying because you're at Bible study!

After replying to say I was getting her messages, she replied — all caps this time — she would call me as soon as she got home. AND PLEASE DO NOT FORGET TO LOCK THE DOORS AND WINDOWS BEFORE YOU SLEEP.

Yes, ma'am.

I put the phone on silent because the messages kept coming — and I was trying to sleep.

But I made sure the doors and windows were locked.

I drifted in and out of sleep — sleeping, but not really asleep — and finally awakened after I was told in a dream that I needed to wake up.

Nothing had prepared me for the sight I awoke to.

My friend was seated on her bed staring at me with a curious look on her face.

Was this a miracle? In one of her messages, my mother had said she would be praying for a miracle.

Was this the answer to her prayers? If it was, why was it not accompanied with joy and rejoicing instead of pure terror?

She looked different, seated on that bed, staring at me.

My phone was flashing, with messages from my mother still coming in. She had called twice after I'd fallen asleep.

I could have just used the buzzer thing in the room, but I didn't like the look on my friend's face. So I said I was going to call the doctor.

I'd listened to my mother and locked the door and windows and now the door wouldn't open.

"I have to tell you something", my friend said.

I mumbled some incomprehensible nonsense and kept trying to open the door. My mind was spinning conspiracy theories, backed up by memories of stories I'd read or heard. And even movies I'd seen.

How does a door just not open? — Unless there's this grand scheme of evil machination you've been caught up in.

This doesn't feel like a miracle at all. Help me, dear Lord. And stop calling me, mother!

****

At first, I thought they must have heard me fiddling with the door — or it was a miracle — but doctors and nurses were all over the place within minutes, attending to my friend.

It turned out my mother had come to the hospital after calling twice and receiving no replies to her messages.

She'd been just in time to hear me fiddling with the door. When she heard my friend's voice, she rushed to get the nurses.

I stood at a corner, transfixed, trying hard to comprehend what just happened.

My friend who had been trying to tell me something only moments ago now lay unconscious again.

Flashing lights and beeping sounds added to the panic that followed. My mother kept trying to find out from nurses what was happening, but we didn't get enough information to allay our worries.

Eventually, we were told she was in a stable condition.

I told my mother about my dream and how I'd woken up to find my friend seated on her bed, staring at me.

"Why didn't you call for them immediately?"She pointed to the buzzer thing, "All you had to do was push a button".

Before I had time to consider if I wanted to let her know my friend had said she needed to tell me something, I heard myself say, "And she said she needed to tell me something".

"What did she say?"

"That she needed to tell me something".

I know when my mother thinks I've been stupid but fights to subdue the right to talk with the will to be a mother.

When she said, "You didn't let her talk", I knew she was doing that fight again, because as hard as she tries, she has not yet mastered the skill of masking pointed sarcasm.

I tried to explain, "The look on her face frightened me".

I should have just kept quiet.

"You weren't taking my calls. You weren't replying my messages. And you weren't letting her talk. Why else do you think they told you in the dream that you needed to wake up?"

She was still doing that fight.

"What look?" She walked over to where my friend lay, "She looks like she's sleeping".

"She was seated on the bed, staring at me—"

"So you didn't let her talk. And now we don't know what she was trying to tell you".

She came back to where I was (I was earnestly pleading with the Lord to help me maintain the peace), "The man that came earlier, he didn't look familiar in any way?"

"No ma'am".

"Nothing was familiar? Nothing about him reminded you of someone you know? Maybe something he said, or something he did?"

I shook my head, "Nothing",

"Or just intuition?"

"I don't know the man—"

Just then, I remembered how he kept looking at his wristwatch. It was almost as if he wanted me to notice it.

"His watch".

"His watch?"

I froze, as the implication hit me. My gaze flitted from my mother to my friend, "I think her husband knows we're here", it was a whisper, but I didn't need to say it twice.

My mother shot up like lightening, "We need to get help", she said, leaving the room — but not before she mentioned the shoddy job I was doing, trying to hide empty cans and bottles. "It's alcohol", she said, "Eventually it would find its way out. It always does".

When she left, I kicked the peeking cans and bottles back under the chair where they were supposed to have been, "I really am trying here".

I really am.

****

Before noon that day, my mother had arranged for us to be transferred to another hospital.

I'd recognise that watch anywhere because I'd gotten it myself. As a joke, my friend had it monogrammed with the first and last letters of the name her husband had begged his mother to stop calling him. When he tired of our taunting, he gifted the watch to a friend.

Was he letting us know he knew where we were?

Were we being watched?

My mother had gotten in touch with my friend's parents. The children were safe. They would handle the situation (with the police and lawyers, and everything). And they were grateful for our help.

On our way home later that day, my mother told me, "You know you can come back home whenever".

When I didn't say anything, she continued, "Please learn from your friend. Learn from the many stories of people who have gone through these things and make their experiences valuable blocks to build with".

If only she knew my plan.

"You don't have to worry about me", I told her, "You won't find me in that condition".

"What would you do? You need a plan—"

If only she knew.

I have a plan.

"Are you listening to me?"

I tried, but I couldn't stop the smile that broke out.

"This is serious—"

I've heard that some smiles are infectious. It must be true because as my smile got bigger, my mother also broke out in one.

I've also heard that until there's the will to do what you decide to do, it remains only a decision. It must be true too... I think....

But I'm about to find out.

4

Just a Little Talk, Chocolate, and a Whole Lot of Common Sense

"This is not a classroom", our music director said, "Put your hand down and sit".

Even I could see he was trying hard, to not get too angry.

It's not like I'd meant to upset him, I just needed to say my piece about the song he had chosen for the annual thanksgiving service at church.

In the course of rehearsing that song, two sopranos had lost their voices. One was certain she had come to the end of her singing days. We tried to help her see that wasn't the case at all. Most rehearsals ended in tears. And we were all convinced that the inspiration for that song could not have come from heaven. But nobody else was going to tell him.

I put my hand down and sat that day, but that was the day I saw a little bit more from my sister's point of view.

Maybe we really could do more…?

I believed she knew what she was doing as she's older than me. So I followed her.

And everything was fine — until I coughed in the middle of a song during a live recording.

✳✳✳

"It was just a stupid, little cough", I told my sister, still trying to get her to see that it wasn't an issue at all, "Just one small cough".

She wasn't on the same page with me though, "One small cough that's now a problem we have to fix".

I seriously do not see what the problem is, here. To cough is not an unnatural thing to do, people!

She must have read my mind, or I might have thought that out loud, because she explained her stance again, "You don't cough in the middle of a song, during a live production".

"It could have happened to anybody".

"But it happened to you".

As the phone began to ring, she waved me away, muttering, as she continued to try to edit the song and hide the cough.

"You could just remove that part of the song".

She let the phone ring and fixed her gaze on me.

Now I've gone and done it! That was never a good sign!

"And replace it with what?"

With that pointed gaze she still aimed my way, it was hard to think of any sensible thing to say but I tried again, "With something similar somewhere else in the recording".

I couldn't tell if she was irritated with me or with the phone that wouldn't stop ringing, but when she said we might need to record that song again if she couldn't at least minimise the cough sounds to a reasonable degree of indistinctness, and I said we could just take the whole song out instead, she said she would tell mama if I didn't stop taking the situation lightly.

That would be a real classy thing for her to do.

I told her so and made a point to take more than she'd usually allow from the basket of sweets on her table — just to get my own back.

"OK, that's it", she squealed, "I'm telling mama!"

Ok, can I just say again that I still think this is a dysfunctional system? I pay that lady, but somehow she thinks it's OK to wave me away when I'm in her office and the phone rings, and run to mama every time I don't agree with her.

Just because she's my manager.

It's true, I coughed in the middle of a song, during a live recording, and somehow everybody thinks it's a problem.

I did my honest best to try to stop it, but it was itchy — the kind of itch that went from your throat to your brain. That couldn't be good. Plus, we were in church. Do they really think it matters all that much that I coughed in the middle of a song while worshipping?

It might have been a live recording, but the goal was to convene a gathering of worshippers who would truly worship.

"Yes", my sister told mama, "Except we had all these people from the Gospel industry that might have been interested in collaborating with us".

"Gospel industry?"

Thank you, mama!

All I wanted to do was sing.

But my sister thought we could do more. Next thing I knew, she was putting videos on YouTube and Facebook. Then we got a website. And a schedule. And then she declared herself my manager.

I told her it didn't feel right, but she said walking into the red sea or the Jordan River must not have felt right for the Israelites at first too. Then she'd preached this homily on how we're supposed to walk by faith, not by sight — or even what we felt.

As she's older than me, I figured she knew what she was talking about.

Then there were contracts and demos, and tours and live recordings — like this very one that's the reason for this present clamouring.

I tried to say one thing from the beginning — all I wanted to do was sing, not have a career in the Gospel music industry.

Pray tell, how is that even a thing?

How did the worship of God get so commercialised that people have to pay to experience it?

And why is it Ok that the notion is even allowed in the Church today?

OK so, I was supposed to be thinking and coming up with ways we could remedy our present predicament — my sister assigned me that task (and I only agreed to do it because it was the only way I could get away from discussing the problem with her. Even though I still didn't think there was one).

I'd told her I could go back to just singing in the choir. She said no.

Do a Facebook post. She did not exactly see the point.

An advertorial. About what?

Write an apology letter. To who?

Forget it ever happened and just keep worshipping....

That's when she assigned me the task and went to tell mama about how lightly I was taking the situation.

****

"We're travelling this evening", my sister announced as she came in the house".

"There's Bible study this evening".

She thought it was a joke that wasn't even funny.

But I wasn't joking.

Some people like to travel — *explore-and-see-the-world* kind of thing. I'm not one of them. I need time to be ready before doing something like that. Plus, there really was Bible study that evening.

And where were we even going? And why?

It turned out she had reached out to an old friend. He was in charge of a citywide thing His church organised annually. This year, some major players in the Gospel industry were involved. And he'd be able to work me into the schedule.

It was supposed to present me with new opportunities.

The only problem was, we had to leave that evening if we'd be there on time.

To my sister, it wasn't a problem, so she made the arrangements before checking to see if it was OK with me.

She's my manager, and that's probably what they do, but still....

Would it have killed her to just ask first? (Not that I would have been that thrilled, but you get the point.)

As she went through the house grabbing things and food, I looked to mama for help. None was forthcoming. She couldn't get over the major players part, and she just kept mentioning it, "You don't know who might discover you".

I reminded her that the annual thanksgiving at church was just weeks away, and I needed to be at rehearsals or they wouldn't let me sing with the choir. She said it was exactly as I'd said — weeks away, and we'd be back in good time.

I thought of running away, but I couldn't think of where to go.

I thought of feigning illness — I even coughed once or twice, but my sister said we'd stop at the hospital to get a prescription.

She was definitely calling my bluff, and the fact just grated on my nerves.

Desperate and not knowing what else to do, I called my pastor's wife.

And then I locked myself in the bathroom.

As we journey through life, the time usually comes when a person stands at a crossroad and has to choose which way to go as he journeys through life.

This was one of those times for me.

I'd had it up to here with over-filtered photos and studio work — and generally, putting up and maintaining appearances. Plus, never being able to just be a normal teenager.

My sister is forever going on about the responsibility that comes with gifting — like, "If God wanted you to be a regular teenager He wouldn't have graced you with this gift".

At first, I thought she must know what she's talking about (since she's older than me), but after the whole experience began to feel more like a burden than a blessing, I began to reconsider that notion.

Why would God want me to sing songs I had no interest in singing, and for just because it was in the genre that was profitable at the time?

And then say things at interviews that were heavily embellished and more than just a tad away from the truth?

And wear clothes I'm not comfortable in — because they make me relatable with the target audience (Ok, I don't even know what that means. Like, really, please!).

I'm just a teenager that wants to sing.

And I was fine singing with the choir at church before my sister came with the videos on YouTube and Facebook. And the website. And the schedule. And declared herself my manager.

So now I was stuck in an industry that's not even supposed to be one in the first place, with a career I didn't even want.

Gospel music industry? What does an oxymoron mean again?

I'm not saying this is all her fault (at least I don't think it's what I'm saying), but when you think about it....

I said I didn't recognise who I'd become, but she said I was too mature for my age.

And it didn't help my cause at all that this whole venture was profitable (monetarily, I mean).

I think I'm done.

As I waited in the bathroom, I was certain something had to give, and fast too, because I didn't think my sister was playing about breaking the door and hauling me in the boot of a car to this event that was supposed to help broaden the scope of our work.

****

It seemed like forever, but my pastor's wife finally came.

After they realised I wasn't playing about staying in the bathroom until my next birthday if I had to, mama had called her. She sounded frantic, "She would starve to death in there. Please come and talk sense into her head".

Then she went on about how I'd inherited my stubbornness from my father and his family.

And about how I had the gift of turning nonissues into life-threatening situations.

And about how she was so worked up now, her eyes were about to fall out because of the severe throbbing in her head.

"Please come before these children kill me. You're the only one she would listen to".

So my pastor's wife had left Bible study to try to restore peace and order — at least that's what I'd thought — and it was the only reason I'd come out from the bathroom.

But then she wasn't pleased I'd tried to give mama a heart attack. *What?* And it wasn't helping that mama was already in tears.

When I said I wasn't hungry, mama began to wail, "She has started with her stubbornness again. She would surely starve herself to death this time".

My sister said there was nothing to worry about, and that I was only being a baby and acting up. She had already packed a bag for me and was now explaining the situation to my pastor's wife.

I stood in a corner, listening. It was as though they were telling the story of my life, and no one bothered to hear from me. As my sister told the story, I interjected from time to time, trying to correct wrong suppositions. My efforts were futile. Apparently, they knew the story of my life better than me.

I had the thought to just up and leave.

And then there was another thought, *Why not?*

Really, why not?

So while they told my story, I upped and left — and they didn't even realise I was gone.

****

My intention was not to cause panic (OK, that might not be completely true), but I was just trying to get them to hear what I'd been trying to say for years.

I didn't go very far. I didn't even leave the compound (as I was only trying to get them to hear me. Plus, I didn't know where else to go).

I thought of going to church, but then they'd get word that I was there, and the whole purpose would have been defeated.

But I got hungry and began to regret not listening to mama when she tried to get me to eat. It helped though, to remember that man does not live by bread alone, and that I may finally have their attention now, after all these years, and it would be foolish to throw that away for some dainty morsels.

As time passed, I almost changed my mind. They were calling uncles and aunties and friends — anyone they could reach, to ask about me. And then some people came over to the house.

My sister was more worried about this opportunity that would now be missed because of my foolishness. When she threatened to stop managing me, a few people told her she ought to be ashamed of herself. "Your younger sister is missing, and you're worried about her career? What is wrong with you?"

Finally! They're beginning to ask the right questions after all these years!

It was decided they'd give it till the next day before reporting to the police. "It's not like it's not something she hasn't done before. And she always comes back".

More people came from church to pray with mama. My pastor's wife and my pastor stayed a bit longer.

And then everyone was gone, with most promising to return the next day, and to keep praying.

My sister was still sulking, probably from the missed opportunity, or from the chiding — but really, what is wrong with her? Her younger sister is missing, and she's worried about a career in the Gospel industry.

After she refused to eat and said she was leaving for a while to think things through, mama was convinced this would be the day she would see the face of Jesus. "They would be orphans if I come now", she told the Lord, "And see how young and stupid they are".

Then she began to plead with the Lord again to keep me safe, and put it in my heart to return, and for my sister to behave like the older child that she's supposed to be and not abandon her in this house at this time.

"Help me Jesus", she prayed, "So that these children do not kill me before my time".

And then she began to wail.

✳✳✳✳

As mama became hysterical, my sister decided against leaving.

For a moment, I thought I was stuck. I'd planned to go back inside after she left, because I wasn't sure what she would do in her fury (and I wasn't exactly looking to take that kind of chance).

57

As night came, so did the mosquitoes. Plus, chilly winds brought drizzling rain with signs that it could get serious. And I was still hungry.

I held out against these conditions as long as I could, and then I decided my point had already been made, and mama would not let my sister deal me any fatal blows.

But I still had to make sure....

As I soon as I found out my sister was in her room, I walked to the house as quietly as I could. The plan was to get what I could from the kitchen and lock myself in my room.

But mama was too excited when I walked in, and made such a fuss, I had to pretend I was still thoroughly vexed as my sister came from her room. Once she was no longer in my way, I bounded for my room and locked the door (I still wasn't taking that chance).

The only problem was that I was still hungry.

Mama begged and cajoled and bribed me to eat. My sister did her bit (She threatened to break down the door and force-feed me to ease mama's worries).

As I unlocked the door, mama rushed in the room, sat on the floor and said if I was trying to go to heaven, then we'd go together.

I thought my sister looked tired, not angry — but I was not ready to confirm that notion.

I walked straight to the kitchen, mama following, probably afraid I'd leave again. I began to look for food. In a matter of minutes, mama had heaped plates and bowls, and was still rummaging through the fridge.

Any other day my sister would have had a fit just seeing what was before me. "You can't eat this". "You can't eat that". "It's bad for your voice". "It would make you fat".

As she joined me at the table, warily eyeing the dainties, mama glared at her, as if to say, "Don't start!"

And then they listened to me tell about how I still didn't think we were doing this thing right. "I just want to sing", I told them, "not put up and maintain appearances, and have a career in an industry that's not even supposed to be one in the first place".

My sister said we could try it differently, but mama told her to let me finish my food.

She put up her hands and left, "Since I'm now the meddler and the cause of all this trouble".

Now I felt for her, because all she had wanted to do was help.

She had always been the go-to person in the family if you wanted something done. She could take a project everyone had given up on and turn it into something that works. And she always sees possibilities and opportunities in every situation.

When I began to be invited to sing at church programs, she thought we needed to get this thing organised.

So she started putting videos on YouTube and Facebook. Then we got a website. And a schedule. And then she declared herself my manager.

Before long we were getting invitations from all over the place and were fully booked for months coming. It didn't take too long after then for the business side to begin to conflict with the essence of what we had set out to do.

As time passed, it became less about the worship and more about honouring contracts and getting new ones — and to do that, you had to stay relevant in the industry — basically, putting up and maintaining appearances.

And that, I no longer wanted to keep doing.

****

Morning came and with it a steady stream of visitors. More than a few wore sullen expressions and came mostly to commiserate with mama. They told tales of runaway teenagers that ended up dead or in serious trouble with the law. "Some even fell into the hands of traffickers", they told mama, "We should be thankful she came to her senses before it was too late".

From the corner where we sat and watched them, my sister and I got tired of feeling sorry for mama because of how annoying her visitors were being (to us, at least). We began to argue about whose fault it was that they were even here in the first place.

She said if I hadn't been such a big baby and acted up, they'd not be here now. I reminded her she had threatened to haul me in the boot of a car for a journey that would have lasted at least six hours.

She said she didn't mean it.

I said I wasn't going to take that chance (after she locked me in my room for one whole day when I ignored her threats to do so if I didn't behave and do my chores, I stopped taking those kind of chances with her).

Eventually, we decided we all had our parts in the unfolding drama.

The problem now was getting them to see there was no grief here — the situation had already been resolved.

As I returned from every counselling session (since they all wanted to have a word with me before they left), my sister would ask me to tell her again whose fault this whole situation was.

When I'd had enough of the sessions, I begged her to help me. I told her mama had had enough too and was just being polite with her visitors. Plus, we were running out of drinks.

"What do you want me to do?"

"Just get this fixed! Please!" I tried to sound as desperate as I could.

She thought I sounded like a toddler caught red-handed with a stolen cookie.

I ignored the comparison as we were in desperate need of her help — mama looked like she was being mobbed.

"So you agree that stupid, little cough created a muddle I needed to fix?"

"Hmm?"

I pointed to mama, "Your mother needs your help!"

She was getting the last laugh again, and all I could do was wait to grow up and be wise like her. She must have been enjoying her position as the older, wiser child. And it came to my mind that the fact just completely annoyed me — not the part about being older and wiser — I could wait! — But she was just plain merciless with her teasing.

I reminded her we already cleared the air about the cough, and the muddle it created, and how we were going to do things differently. She would still be my manager, but we would do our best to see that the business side of things does not conflict with the worshipping that we had set out to do from the beginning. And I could rehearse with the choir at church, so they'd let me sing with them at the annual thanksgiving. "Now please go save mama!"

She told me to stop sulking and come with her.

I didn't think it was a good idea, and I told her so.

When she began to lay out plans and strategies, I began to wonder if leaving the house had been a good idea — I didn't even leave the compound or go very far, but see all the drama we've had to deal with in the hours following. And we were still receiving more visitors.

I told my sister she could pass a note to mama and tell her to meet us in the car. We could go on that journey now, for the event her friend was in charge of.

She said my problem is that I never take anything seriously.

****

Looking back, I'd say it all worked out well.

We learned lessons — like, when mama has visitors eager to make a point of being there for her, never interrupt with the flimsy excuse of needing to talk to your mama — unless you can do so with a straight face (and also, unless you're trying to win a bet).

Now I have to do the dishes for a week, but at least it worked, and it was better than all the crazy schemes and strategies my sister had come up with.

We also decided on new ways we could do things — like, getting filled first before trying to pour into others. Worship is first a spiritual exercise before anything else, and if we must worship, we must do so in spirit and in truth. And, how can we know the truth if we won't make the effort to find it?

So we'd be taking personal and family devotions more seriously. I won't be running away from the house when I'm upset (because it upends mama's world, and that is never a good thing). And my sister wouldn't be making threats that cause me to be irrational and start doing things like running away from the house when I'm upset, and upending mama's world....

Mama always says just a little talk, chocolate, and a whole lot of common sense can get anything fixed.

It must be true, because all we had to do was have a *come-to-Jesus* meeting with chocolate, and a whole lot of common sense. And now this situation is completely resolved. For now, at least.

5

Redeeming Lost Time, Making All Things Beautiful in His Time

I awoke to a sound I hadn't heard in a while — like half a century, maybe.

Wind blowing, leaves rustling, with birds frantic to get to their nests. The pitter-patter of raindrops on the roof and windows completed the medley. I tried to be still, afraid any sudden movements would bring it all to an end.

It wasn't the first rainy day in like half a century.

It wasn't the first time since then that the wind, rustling leaves, frantic birds and pitter-pattering raindrops would work together in perfect harmony.

I was just a person with little people that needed my attention all day as I was the chief finder of things including, but not limited to missing toys, socks, favourite books and unfinished snacks — things I had to fish out from unthinkable places. I would do you the favour of sparing you the dreary details, but do feel sorry for me because these hands have been places and these eyes have beheld disturbing sights, so much so that I've been awakened from countless nightmares featuring toys stuck in unlikely places, missing unfinished breakfasts the preacher's wife found tucked away in the crevice of some sofa after three whole days of turning the house upside down, in search of the elusive breakfast, and after having come to the decision to wait out the stench. And there was the recurring nightmare of pulling out dried frogs from my purse at work.

I was also the chief dishwasher, cook, nurse, transporter, dictionary, and encyclopaedia.

The cleaner and fixer of things, and basically, the person whose job it was to give the house a semblance of where humans live.

And then someone had to figure out how to get money because there were bills to pay.

It had to be me too because as my preteen daughter reminded me one time, I was the adult in the house. It's what adults do. And I was supposed to get with the program.

Say what now, child? Believe me, I saw different shades of red, stars and rage.

Somehow, it was easy to miss that perfect harmony of the wind, rustling leaves, frantic birds and pitter-pattering raindrops working together.

Somewhere between birthdays, school plays, children's day, Christmas carols, and mothers' day every once in a while, when I let them get away with things they know they'd be in trouble for (like when I returned from a trip and found the car needing major bodywork) the years rolled by and my littles flew the coop before I even knew it was time.

All I have left are memories — at least that's what I'm supposed to have. And I do my best to take hold of what I can.

Memories — like when I told the offending child after the car incident that we had to come up with a plan to cover the cost of fixing the car if college would still be in the picture for her.

Well… let's just say it was in everybody's interest that I had waited until after mother's day to lay this out because the whole mothers' day plan that had been months in the making would have been sabotaged, as it was years after then before she understood why getting another job was the better option.

For years I'd tried to explain it was either that or foregoing college, or else she'd be subjecting the whole family to subsisting on cheap bread with no milk, eggs, or meat for at least twenty years. We simply did not have that much margin.

It wasn't until she had children of her own though, that she saw my point.

Sometimes, I feel like I'm grasping the wind. At other times I'm sure I'm grasping at straws.

It was like the more I tried to do right, the more the rules kept changing.

I read all the books on motherhood I could find and only stopped studying the Proverbs 31 lady after my eldest turned thirty-four. I stayed up late every Tuesday reading all the magazines and journals I could find, but for some reason, those time-tested principles didn't apply to our family.

Discipline them, the books said, so I did. They began to develop secret lives and embrace vices to protest the rules. The books said it was to be expected, and that it meant we were on the right track. After one of them was caught shoplifting so he could raise money to pay a classmate to help with homework, and another was called to the Principal's office after she wrote an essay on how she spent her Christmas holiday that year, I decided we might have gone a bit too far with that rule.

It was nearly the same thing with the *your-children-are-not-your-friends-they're-you're-children* rule. They said they already knew I was the enemy.

My goal was to see that they had a roof over their heads.

That, and putting food on the table, clothes on their backs, and basically doing my best to supply the needs they had — needs that grew in proportion to their years — and there was more than one of them. As in, children, more than one child.

It felt like an endless struggle with no end in sight.

There were many days, and all those mornings, dragging my sleep-deprived self around town with fidgety littles in tow. There were times I lost my temper and yelled at them at church, and also, the times I didn't feel bad about dropping them off at school after holidays. I was the mom squealing tires and in a hurry to get out of the school parking lot before they change their mind and tell me to come get my kids. So while other moms were feeling bad, some even crying, about having to be apart from their kids until school lets out, I felt bad about not feeling bad.

I tried to share my frustration, but it wasn't all that helpful.

I was told I was the perfect example of what a bad mother is. Others said I would get what was coming to me when I get old and my children dumped me at the worst home for seniors they could find and never return.

There were more than a few though who said I was doing OK, but they were nearly crowded out.

And the years just flew by.

It wasn't all thorns and no roses, though. I would be the first to affirm that somehow, we did find our way, even though it wasn't exactly where we had in mind when we began this journey — a journey we didn't know much about at first, and still don't fully understand.

Because, when you think about it, who really does have life completely figured out?

I did reach my goal, but not without the help of fellow travellers — friends, family and total strangers who chose to lend a hand.

There was always a roof over my children's heads, food on the table, clothes on their backs, and those proportionate needs were being supplied, but only because people stood in places I couldn't.

They watched the children while I went to work. They gave anonymous gifts so we could celebrate birthdays. They prayed with us, brought us food and helped us see truth again when it was being blurred out by the haze that sometimes comes with the endeavour to live.

It took me about half a century, but I did reach my goal.

But it wasn't without a prize.

I missed opportunities to be present, and impact my children in ways that could spur them on to traverse these spheres sensibly, with the advantage of a mother's experience. And every child has a story to tell with regards to these misses.

But I did try to explain.

I needed to work to reach my goal.

And I needed to be away to work.

When they were younger, it was easy for them to understand. You'd think they'd grow wiser as they grew older, and get it, especially as they all have children of their own now.

But no—

They got stuck in that time when they started to believe I abandoned them in order to pursue my goals, build castles on earth, and make a fortune for myself.

Now they ask me if I reached my goals, where the castles are, and if I made that fortune for myself.

Having walked down this road, I know now that I would do some things differently — but not that differently.

My goal would still be the same (and it was just one, when you think of it). It was to take care of my children.

✳✳✳✳

So these past ten years I've been in a facility for the elderly, run by fine Christians who help make the burden lighter.

I did find God eventually, and I believe He directed my steps to this place. I know now that I was never really all alone all those years.

Ten years ago, I decided I was done, and overdosed on antidepressants. I woke up in the hospital and my church family wouldn't let me go back home alone.

As I had no idea how to reach my children or any other family member that might still be alive, they cajoled me into my present living situation (one or two threatened me with something, and even though I had no idea what they were talking about, they sounded like they weren't playing).

I've heard that there are more than a few ways to find your family these days, but the details are all so overwhelming. I deferred to the cajoling and threatening.

It turned out to be a blessing.

I've made new friends and found a new purpose. Now I tell people about my journey and admonish them to choose wisely.

Most days are good, but there are still those other days where it seems like we're back where we started.

I miss my children. I want to know that they're OK.

All I have left are those memories, and pictures of them from when they still let me take family photos.

It had been one of those days, and I'd fallen asleep going through those pictures before I awoke to the sound of that perfect harmony.

It was a shower of blessing coming down in his season, sent from heaven, just for me.

It was a rebirth.

A reawakening.

A rediscovery of what used to be.

As I sat and listened, I remembered.

There used to be a time before we got busy and tried to reach goals (even singular goals that involved supplying the needs of children).

There used to be a place where the simple things were more than enough for us.

I'd reckon to find our way back to that time and place, we need to get to the feet of Jesus. We'd need to be still there — to be quiet, and just listen.

When Jesus said *"I am the way"*, that was exactly what He meant.

Did you do all you could, and work through the situation with integrity?

Did you find the way to God yet?

Let's hope, and have faith in Him.

Let's trust that He would make all things beautiful in His time.

As I sit and listen, I earnestly hope that He would because I want to see my children and my grandchildren, and tell them about this new purpose I've found. They might already know parts of the story, but I want to tell them about my journey, and admonish them to choose wisely.

And I want to tell them about the fortune I made for myself.

Even though it doesn't matter very much to me now (because the attainment of temporary and fleeting gains pale greatly in contrast to what really counts in the grand scheme of things) I did make that fortune. And I built those castles.

I have now been left with the responsibility of dispensing reliefs to fellow travellers who need a hand.

The knowledge that by my efforts (no matter how meager) some mama's distress is being eased, does its bit, though not quite fully, to ease the weight of this old mama's burden of lost time, opportunities, and children.

I've been reminded again that there's hope yet, and all is not completely lost. It may be true, who knows?

Because some things are always true (or at least they stay true for a long time). Like how after all these years, it still does take a village to raise a child.

So maybe it's true, and all is not completely lost.

It's harder to know on some days, like today.

But today, I will be content, listening to the sound of that perfect harmony.

I did do what I could, working through my situation with integrity — that has to be counting for something, somewhere.

6

Vacationing in Paris

Somebody, come get this child! Please!!!! Anybody!?!

It was my fourth Facebook post in one day.

At first, I'd asked if anyone wanted to keep both children for the weekend. Then I'd asked if they'd keep them for only a few hours. And then I'd asked if they'd keep just the granddaughter?

She wouldn't stop shrieking like a banshee!

I'd bring food and money! Just take the child! My posts got massive amounts of reactions and comments, but no takers.

As I hardly ever do more than read comments and memes on Facebook, by the fourth post, I was done posting. The last shreds of hesitancy to call our present situation by its proper name finally gave way, and the fact was cemented in my mind that these were desperate times.

Our daughter was in Paris with her husband pretending she had no children, while I was saddled with the responsibility of chasing two toddlers around the house and wiping pee from my recliner at least twice a day.

"See how this child is pushing all my buttons the wrong way and trying to get me to do what we talked about this morning?" I told the Lord as I wiped pee from the recliner for the second time again, one day, "I'm trying to not get out of control but I'm too old to be doing this".

And she's too old to be doing this, too.

I know, she's my granddaughter, and she's a reasonable child — at least she acts like it — sometimes, but still....

After two whole weeks of chasing them down, trying to keep them from killing themselves or setting the house on fire, I was ready to start pulling my hair out.

Bless the husband's heart! Because I'm not sure what might have been had he not taken the grandson out today for a *boys day out bonding-ish kind of thing.*

When I had children, they were nothing like what we have today. Either that, or I'm just getting old.

In case I've not already been clear enough—

My grandchildren terrify me.

No, I wouldn't trade them for anything else in the world, but still....

Seriously, please—

I do not need an audience when I go to the bathroom.

Three comes after two, and before four.

Ice cream and popcorn is not a proper dinner.

And how can two little people make such a mess, you pray for a miracle and exercise your faith every time you clean up after them?

I don't know where they get all that energy, but help me, Jesus! Please!

The husband has said the running around is good for our backs. Well, going by how difficult it's getting for both of us to get out of bed these days, I seriously doubt that.

And we're always needing balm to massage someplace. So now we're stocking up on balm like milk and gravy. This shouldn't be happening. We're not that old.

Again, he's said it's good for the family — mending fences and all.

I have to admit, I was more than a little surprised when my daughter called to ask if the children could stay with us while she and her husband went on vacation to Paris.

"Sure, no problem". I was pleased we could be of help. Grateful, even.

"How long would you be gone?"

Not that we would have changed our minds if it was for more than a few days, but still.…

We hadn't heard from them in a while — a while like more than seven years. And then out of nowhere she calls and asks for this favour.

I didn't even know she had a daughter.

With the first child, I found out on Facebook and tried to reach out. She blocked me.

Believe me, I cried for fourteen days straight. Nonstop. Then I picked myself up and said "Never again".

At first, she'd said they'd be gone for two weeks. Then after they'd been gone a week, she called to say they'd be a month.

And was I livid!

I said we were being taken for granted.

The husband said she was reaching out, trying to mend fences.

Please! She blocked me, her own mother, on Facebook. Who does that?

Reaching out, trying to mend fences? I didn't think so. I may have stated my point a tad too strong because he finally reminded me, "She's our only child".

Twang! Something must have given way inside because the rage that emanated from me in that moment terrified even me. Bless God it was on a Wednesday evening. The husband left for Bible study, even though it was a full hour early.

I didn't think I could go to church with all that rage. It was ugly.

The husband didn't think so. He said something about God already being here, and all our ways are before Him. And we can't hide from Him. And He's the only one who can help us. And we need to run to Him, not from Him at all times, no matter what.

I thought he was preaching to me — because it sounded like he was, but when I asked him, he said he wasn't preaching. He was just telling me the truth.

I'd try to keep this simple—

That statement about telling me the truth increased the rage by mega decibels.

He could have just said "Yes, I'm preaching to you right now". Because that's what he was doing.

There was no way this prodigal child of mine was going to make me cry again, so I ate a whole tub of ice cream and binge-watched really bad TV shows so I could take my rage out on how poorly they were made. When I finally started to cry, I knew it was because my weight loss program had been set back again. When would I ever fit into that dress hanging in my wardrobe, my motivation for losing weight? It's been in my wardrobe for four years.

I told the husband that was enough to make a woman cry.

He didn't believe it.

He said something about it being time to stop being in denial and acknowledge my grief.

OK get this—

I don't even know what that means.

He can believe whatever he wants, but I know I wasn't crying because of that prodigal child of mine.

OK, so that's how we found ourselves with two toddlers—

After our prodigal daughter shows up out of nowhere, after seven years of absolutely no communication, and leaves them with us, while she went to Paris with her husband, pretending she didn't have any children.

They're taking selfies at the Eiffel tower and eating hors d'oeuvres at fancy restaurants that could make you forget the dress hanging in your wardrobe (your motivation for losing weight), while I'm here changing nappies, chasing down toddlers and cleaning pee from my recliner at least twice every day.

And no, I'm not vain like that, I'm just saying….

The husband says I need a change in perspective, or some twelve-step program.

I say he's just jealous because his granddaughter is terrified of him.

He says mine is a classic case of denial, and I need Jesus.

I say he has no idea what he's talking about. I already have Jesus. How else does he think we've survived with the children these two weeks?

Now to go get lunch started, and quiet the shrieking banshee.

To find the bottle of aspirin, and quiet this gnawing suspicion that the husband may be right again this time.

Because then, what am I going to do?

****

I believe the fault was mine.

I'd fallen asleep trying to read my Bible.

And I'd fallen asleep on *that* recliner.

Two missteps of gargantuan proportions.

Because next thing I know, I'm being peed on.

I do need the Word of God.

I acknowledge this need and I do my best to get in the habit of being in the Word.

We've been told it's not that hard to do.

Just show up.

Study.

Be a hearer and a doer of the Word.

I'd say it's easier said than done, but then again, it might be just my own experience.

The husband makes the effort, and it seems to me like he's reaping the benefits.

He's never so stressed that he's ready to fall apart.

He's always at peace.

And then there's that wisdom and quiet confidence he exudes all day, every day.

I could have been jealous, but he's the husband, and sometimes I partake in these benefits — like when the bills are already due, and the money is still on its way. Or when your prodigal daughter drops her children on you so she can go to Paris with her husband and pretend she doesn't have children, while you're falling asleep trying to read the Bible, and getting peed on because you'd fallen asleep on that recliner (the one I have to wipe pee from, at least twice every day).

So yes, the fault was mine. I should have stayed away from that recliner, knowing how much my granddaughter just loves to pee on it (who would ever know why?)

And I shouldn't have fallen asleep.

I don't know how they do it, but there are people who stay in the Word and pray like we're supposed to. You'd know by how well put together they and their lives are.

I'd know, because I live with one. Even though he'd never admit it.

He says it's a matter of perspectives.

I say it's easy for him to say, "She didn't block you on Facebook".

"I don't have Facebook".

OK, so that should count for something, but still….

She didn't block him.

That fault too could be mine.

I should have stayed away when she told me to, not flood her inbox with emails. And leave countless voicemails. And send endless cards (with those books about how prodigals can find their way back home, and why they need to do it soon).

Then there were all those prayers to God. Looking back now, I see how I wasn't even asking for anything. I'd mostly been telling God to see what she had done when we hadn't wronged her in any way. We had done everything right, and I told God so.

But what if the husband is right, and it's truly a matter of perspectives? Or worse, what if there's grief I need to acknowledge?

I'd take the twelve-step program, Please! For anything they're trying to fix (anything but what the husband thinks, that is).

Because where would I begin?

How did I even get here?

How did our family get this beaten?

How can we make it better?

And what has been my role in all of this?

Too many questions with answers that seem very out of reach.

And so, somehow I find I'm back to this very place—

I need the Word of God, and a bit of balm for my back, and some aspirin, because of this shrieking granddaughter of mine....

I don't know what the deal is with all that shrieking. Like, it was she who peed on me while I was minding my own business. But then again, since I fell asleep on *that* recliner reading my Bible, it was probably all my fault....

Especially when you remember that I picked up my Bible in the first place because she wouldn't stop singing "Read your Bible, pray every day, if you want to grow...."

(OK, I don't know what she was singing, but it was to the tune of that very song, so....)

Dear Lord! This situation just makes my whole head spin.

I need to find that bottle of aspirin....

✳✳✳✳

It turned out I was right.

She called again after three weeks to say they'd be gone for two months.

"Something came up, but I can't discuss it now".

Wait.... We're stuck with your kids. You invaded our lives, but you don't think we need to know what's going on? Well, I don't think so!

The husband must have seen the wheels turning in my head because he hijacked the conversion before I'd had the chance to say my mind.

Remember the benefits thing I mentioned earlier? Of what I partake in because the husband spends time in the Word? At times like this, I'm not so sure!

It's probably part of it though because I definitely would not have handled the situation the same way.

Got my point already?

I was spoiling for war.

Don't get me wrong, I adore my grandchildren, and I'm grateful for the chance I've had to get to know them, but still….

And no, I'm not vain like that.

And I'm not a terrible person.

I just plain have a hard time dealing with being taken for granted.

So here's the story she was selling—

She went to Paris with her husband because they're trying to work on their marriage and find better job opportunities.

And these things, they couldn't do at home?

I wasn't buying that story. I thought something was fishy. And that's what I told the husband.

He thought I was reading too much into the situation.

After days of trying to get him to see my point (I may or may not have nagged him to the point of exasperation), he finally let me explain my view.

I told him I thought they might be in trouble with the law. They're young and brash and have probably done something stupid.

"Like what?" He sounded more like he was trying to determine the state of my mind more than he wanted to know the answer to that question.

"I don't know", I was trying to not give him a reason to believe I was paranoid. But I wanted him to know, "Maybe they siphoned money from the company where she works".

"How?"

Duh! "With a computer".

OK, so now he thought I was crazy.

He went back to reading the newspaper. He wouldn't continue the conversation. And for days he regarded me like he was sorry for me.

And I was going to let him know I hadn't gone and lost my own mind. I was going to get proof.

I scoured Facebook and YouTube for days, searching for proof or anything that could point me in the right direction.

Something about their story wasn't adding up, and my gut feeling was that my baby was in trouble.

Maybe not with the law, but still in trouble anyway.

And what's a momma to do, especially when the husband thinks my imagination is getting the better of me again!

Needless to say, Facebook and YouTube didn't help very much. I try, but I still don't get the hang of social media. They keep shaking things up every time you think you've got it.

So my searches came up empty. And, I kept getting distracted by all those cute babies, cats, and dogs videos and memes.

Maybe now would be a good time to pray?

And maybe read my Bible…?

As soon as I get my shrieking banshee to be quiet, and find the bottle of aspirin, and figure out why the grandson is always so quiet around me.

Now that I think of it, he's always looked spooked around me.

****

I'm just a nana doing her best with her grandchildren.

I know I deal with my own brand of weirdness, but don't we all?

Still, I think something's off with the way my grandson is terrified of me, and my granddaughter starts shrieking, and you can't even tell why.

I can't shake off the feeling that my daughter needs my help.

And I can't get the husband to see that I'm not imagining things.

I still pray and try to spend time in the Word. Even though on most days even I know I should be doing better, I try to make the effort. Like, I even downloaded audio versions of the Bible, and try to listen. I'll admit though that I fall asleep listening, but still....

Some days I think about my family and the thought comes to me that I might be reaping the reward of some seed I'd sown earlier.

Maybe it's true, because we've been told that we would reap whatever we sow. And one time the preacher said we can't sow bad seeds and go home and pray for crop failure. We would reap what we sow because God is not mocked.

Other days the thought comes to me that I'm being punished for some sin I'd sinned against God.

Maybe it's true, because it's hard to make sense of all we have to deal with as a family.

And then there are those days when the thought comes to me that all God requires of me is faithfulness, and even when I fail, there's grace, plenty. And tomorrow is always a better day because of God's steadfast love and mercies that are new every morning.

Maybe it's true?

The husband always says if God's children would believe Him as eagerly and wholeheartedly as we believe the lies of the enemy, we'd know His grace and power in ways that even this ungodly world cannot deny.

Maybe it applies to our family's situation?

Or maybe I'm reaping the reward of some seed I'd sown earlier?

Or I'm being punished for some sin I'd sinned against God?

If only I could tell which it was… and discover why more and more my grandchildren seem to me like they're fearful children.

So just when I'd almost given up on making sense of anything, I get a call from my daughter's best friend. They'd been friends since they were children, and they had kept in touch.

Any other day, I would have been almost sick with rage. When my daughter had said she had moved on and didn't want anything to do with her past, I'd thought she'd meant ANYTHING. Now we're finding she meant just us, as she was obviously still in touch with friends from that same past.

Maybe I just could no longer care that much anymore. Or maybe I truly could make an exception for this friend — she had always been a sweet girl. Whatever it was, I was surprised to find I didn't care all that much.

And I couldn't tell if it was a pleasant surprise or not.

So the friend wanted to talk, and the urgency I sensed in her voice made me agree to meet with her immediately.

She'd happened upon some information and believed my daughter might be in trouble.

Aha!

Mother always knows — people, spread the word, and let the world know that mother always knows — and I'm not just saying!

But this wasn't the time to do my victory dance.

"The police might be involved by now", she was probably trying to not cause me to go into shock, but I could tell from her demeanour that there was more. So I prodded until she told me, "And she didn't even leave the country in the first place".

Now I had to do my honest best to keep from going into shock.

Would balm help with something like that?

Or aspirin, maybe?

I might have wheezed a bit. Or it might have been the sound of the wheels turning in my head, but she offered me water and waited for me to regain my composure.

I told her she was wrong on the count of my daughter not leaving the country, "She's been calling us and I've seen the country code".

"She could call you from here and make it look like she's calling from Paris".

"With a computer?" I've heard computers do a lot of things.

She tried to explain how that could happen, but a lot of what she said went over my head. When she offered to do a demonstration, I knew she knew what she was talking about.

But why was all of this happening?

I had to tell the husband. This whole turn of events was a lot to process. And I told her that. I could sense though that time was of the essence, and whatever we had to do, we needed to begin immediately.

On a whim, I asked her if my grandchildren had always been so fearful.

"Children?"

"I thought you kept in touch?"

"Yes ma'am, but before the last two months since she disappeared and went off everybody's radar, she had one child".

I was confused and made no attempt to hide the fact.

And she must have sensed it, "I practically raised that boy, babysitting him. I would know".

Dear Jesus, help me!

Is this child lying to me?

I know she's sweet and all, but does the capability to hurt not lie inherent in even sweet girls? I know I read that somewhere. I couldn't be making something like this up.

Except I'm starting to lose my mind….Or I just need to wake up and find that this has all been a terrible dream….

Or maybe find the bottle of aspirin.

✳✳✳✳

We agreed to meet the next day, with the husband this time. She thought she might know where my daughter was, "She needs all the help she could get at this time".

After I relayed the outcome of our meeting to the husband, he said we needed to tread this ground carefully. Translated, that would be, "Stay home and watch the grandchildren while I go with the friend to try to make sense of what's going on with our daughter".

I know about being submissive as a wife and all, but what was I supposed to do with all the emotions raging within? Like, I couldn't even trust me with myself, more so these children, especially as one might not even be my grandchild — not that I'd hold that against the shrieking banshee, but still….

"The pastor's wife wouldn't mind babysitting them while we're gone, if that's what you're concerned about". Of course, it wasn't! I just couldn't come up with a better argument at that moment.

He nearly choked on his tea, spraying it all over the kitchen floor I'd just mopped not quite five minutes earlier. Story of my life!

And it wasn't helping that he was staring at me like I'd grown another head, or I had spaghetti from last night's dinner in my hair again.

"What?" I ran my hand through my hair (OK, it was so tangled, it seemed more like I dragged my hand through my hair) trying to make sure the spaghetti thing didn't happen again.

"Why would the pastor's wife want to babysit the kids?"

Seriously? Like really? "Because she's the pastor's wife, and she tries to be there for us when we need her".

There was that stare again, "Give me that number", he handed me his cell phone so I'd program it in, "I'd let you know how it goes".

It was more than a few things that ran through my mind to say to him in that moment — and most of them were heavily embellished with words that weren't very righteous.

And it took a while for my mouth which had been hanging open the whole time I was trying to behave properly and not spit out those embellishments, to snap back shut

I handed him my cell phone and got the mop, "She's the last person who called".

Then I took the rage out on my poor kitchen floor. I know! — It didn't deserve it, but it was better than pouring all that rage on a person. Plus, I had no idea what to do with the thoughts that began to assault my mind.

It was the swiftness with which they came, I think. And it didn't help that I had no answers to the questions.

Why does everyone think you're the problem when situations come up? Why don't they involve you when they start to work through the situations? Why does nobody trust you to do anything really important, things that really count for something? How does spaghetti always end up in your hair? And why do people find your idea of who a pastor's wife is, incredulous?

It must have been one of those days because for a moment I truly believed the problem was me.

I was about to sit on my kitchen floor and bawl my eyes out when my phone rang. It was the pastor's wife. Ha!

Then the shrieking banshee awoke for the day.

Her screams must have terrified the grandson who took what he could from his breakfast plate and ran to hide behind the kitchen door.

I have to tell you that thoroughly perplexed me.

And then the pastor's wife said she was coming over, "To talk".

I know she's the pastor's wife, and I have my own ideas of what that means. And coming over, just to talk is not part of the picture in my head. Maybe it's just me, but still….

The day could only go two ways from that point — get better, or I'd be left with the task of trying to unravel the massive knots that had formed in my stomach.

Lord, help me!

It turned out the husband had gone straight to the pastor after he left. They had decided it was best not to leave me to my own devices, especially as I had the grandchildren with me. So they got the pastor's wife. She was supposed to help me keep it together until the men got back.

Even if it's just me saying it, she did have her work cut out for her that day.

By the time she stood at my door, I was already a mess and completely convinced that my only escape was hiding in my bathroom until the nightmare was over.

Thankfully, she was at my door before I made it to the bathroom.

She looked so out of place in the jumbled mess my house had become in the months the grandchildren had been with us. At first, I'd followed them around, cleaning up after them. But it didn't take very long to realise I couldn't keep up with them. So now, as long as it won't burn down the house or cause anyone to slip, fall and break their back or lose teeth, I just leave it alone.

I apologised for the way the house looked — at least I tried, but she wouldn't let me. She said she's been a pastor's wife for nearly half a century. And honestly, I couldn't make the connection. But after she started pushing things aside instead of asking where they were supposed to be, I knew she must have lived this same life.

The shrieking banshee became fast friends with her. And the grandson too.

I had thoughts come in my mind that bordered on paranoia….

But seriously, think about it, she's not their nana, yet they wanted to sit with her and let her feed them and play with them. They didn't fuss all that much if they wanted something and she said no. The grandson didn't look one bit terrified of her, and the only time the granddaughter screamed was when I tried to sit with them as she read them a story from the Bible.

But… who seriously reads from the book of Jeremiah to children?

If they were trying to make me jealous, their efforts were yielding bountiful harvests.

It must have been the paranoia thing, but I thought they preferred her to me, and they probably wished she was their nana instead of me, since she was obviously a better one than me. And she clearly made them happy. Although their smiles seemed more like smirks to me when it was directed my way, as if to say, you should take a page from her book and learn something.

I feed them popcorn and ice cream — what more could have been done for these little people?

It turned out she was good with weary nanas too.

As I sat and sulked, trying to understand why my grandchildren were being such little traitors, she came and sat with me, and asked if we could pray because—

"You look terrible",

I feel terrible, thank you! I dared not make that admission to her hearing because I wasn't really looking forward to an hour-long sermon on faith and the miracles of God. And I truly believed she would give it.

She smiled what seemed like a knowing smile and began to sing.

I checked to see what the grandchildren were doing behind us. Everyone knows it's never good when children are unusually quiet. They were being civil with each other and quietly going through one of the picture books I could never get them to look at. I had given up and thought them not fascinated with books as I could never get them to be still long enough and not make a fuss when it came time to read them stories.

So yes, I was more than a little bit surprised, "What did you do?"

"They must like that book a lot", she said, laughing.

Right… I've lived with them long enough to know they can't stand books.

Or maybe it's me they can't stand.

Believe me, I didn't think that second thought by myself, but just as I began to consider it, and see how it might be true, she took my hands and began to pray for me.

It stopped me dead in my tracks, and I could no longer fully process that thought.

She prayed for the peace of God that passes all understanding to fill my heart and home till it overflowed.

She prayed for miracles.

And for us to be grounded in the truth God has already spoken about us.

The relief I felt in that moment was more than what any quantities of aspirin could give.

And for the first time in a while, I truly believed that God was here. He would visit us, and we would truly be OK.

Sometimes I wonder what John the Baptist must have felt as he sat in jail, imprisoned for speaking the truth. He had preached Jesus as the Christ, the long-awaited Messiah who was supposed to bring freedom. He sent his disciples to ask Jesus if He was the Messiah they had been expecting.

I wonder about the prophet Isaiah sometimes too. He was faithful in his calling. He told the people what God told him to tell them, yet no one believed him. To those who didn't know any better, his ministry might have seemed to them a colossal failure, and a succinct example of how not to do ministry.

And then there was the prophet Jeremiah too, imprisoned for telling the truth.

And the disciples and early believers too….

My point?

Just because God's in it doesn't mean there wouldn't be challenges. And just because there are challenges, it doesn't mean God's not in it.

If only we'd remember this truth more — and especially when we need it (OK, usually we do remember, but allow fear, doubt and anxiety cloud our good sense so much, it starts to look like we don't even know these things in the first place).

So just when I started to believe that we were OK, the men came back empty — at least that's how it looked to me.

The friend had been right. My daughter had in fact, never left the country. And they had missed her by a hair's breadth. They were told she had left the hotel only minutes before they got there.

If only I'd been heard when I first said something was off about the whole situation, and my baby could be in trouble — Mother always knows — Why is that hard to get?

And what is the friend not letting on?

I thought she looked squeamish as she sat on the edge of the chair.

The husband kept trying to reassure her. He told her it wasn't her fault, and she did what we could. The pastor expressed our gratitude. The pastor's wife brought her water when she asked for it. And the husband kept trying to deflect the laser beams from my eyes I aimed at her.

Not that I blamed her, or held anything against her, I just wished she'd let us know sooner what she was trying to keep from us. The information could be useful. You'd think she'd know that — except she was trying to protect herself or her interests, maybe....

Seeing as we had hit a dead-end and might be running out of time in what was starting to look like a curious situation, the husband and the pastor decided it was best to inform the police.

And again, they wouldn't let me go with them.

But the friend could go. Ugh! The things a submissive wife has to do!

I made one more plea.

I told the friend to consider the possibility that my daughter might not only be in trouble but also in danger. I begged her to tell us where she believed my daughter might be headed. Her guess didn't have to be correct, but it could make a way out of the quagmire we'd landed in.

It couldn't be only me who had no idea what was going on. Or how the hope we had held just a while ago was slipping through our hands like grains of sand, and there was nothing we could do, except pray and keep hoping.

Why was she so afraid?

Why did our daughter leave her children with us and lie about leaving the country?

And why won't the grandson come out from where he'd been hiding since he saw the friend? The moment he saw her, he had run behind a chair and refused to come out. The granddaughter was thoroughly agitated too, and not even the pastor's wife with all her charms could help this time.

Something was definitely off.

Something we'd be needing more than balm and aspirin to deal with.

How could no one else see this?

This was one of those times to remember truth again — just because these challenges have arisen, it doesn't mean God is not here, helping us, right?

****

The friend finally told us.

She had no idea where my daughter was, but she could be in danger because she had crossed some really powerful people.

I felt sorry for her now because she looked like she was about to come apart.

What was she so afraid of?

Good thing saner minds were there to handle the situation. I might have let my trepidation get the better of me.

Around the time my daughter brought the kids over, she had just found out that the children's home she worked at was giving the children out for money, in a manner of speaking.

To the outsider and even those who volunteered there, like my daughter, their cause seemed like a noble one. They were supposed to help take care of these children who had nowhere else to go. There was a well mapped out legal and ethical framework for families wanting to adopt, and it could take a while to complete the process. But children soon began to disappear. They gave reasons and tried to dispel the misgivings of those who asked questions.

We've been told that nothing is hidden forever. It must be true because it wasn't too long before they found it hard to keep up with the stories they had to come up with, to cover their tracks.

My daughter believed something was off and started digging. The more she found out, the more she realised how much danger she could be in because of how much she knew.

After she was found in possession of a file that was supposed to be top secret, she knew the bubble had burst. Her husband didn't think they should all sail in one boat, so he convinced her to bring the grandchildren over.

She had come up with the vacation story because she didn't want too many people to know where they were — and we'd be telling the truth if we ever got questioned, and we said we didn't know where they were.

She had kept in touch with the friend (until the last few hours, at least) because, well, some things just do not turn out as intended.

The granddaughter was technically not my granddaughter. She was to be given out to a couple my daughter didn't trust. So my daughter took off with her, brought her and the grandson over, and disappeared.

"Wait, so you're saying we're accomplices to the stealing of a child?"

"She did good ma'am! Those children are severely maltreated".

"But my daughter stole a child that's with me right now."

For the life of me, I couldn't tell how everybody else was hearing those same words and not coming apart at the seams like I was.

Probably trying to justify what my daughter did, she went on to describe how badly the children were treated at the home. They were poorly fed, and the younger ones were usually medicated to get them to sleep when they wouldn't stop crying.

And the matron was a terror to the children.

She was never gentle with them. She barked orders and was always too willing to hit them.

The grandson had been around the matron long enough to be terrified of her, but not long enough to tell the difference between us....

Yes, I just found out why the grandchildren are usually alarmed around me—

I look like said matron.

Dear Lord! This story just keeps getting better.

So in a matter of only hours, I went from being a regular nana to being in custody of a stolen child. It doesn't help that like a broken record, it keeps playing in my mind that we might be on the wrong side of the law. Also, I look like some mean matron at a shady children's home.

Just some hours ago, my biggest challenge had been trying to read my Bible without falling asleep. Well, that and wiping pee from *the* recliner, and keeping the grandchildren from burning down the house or killing themselves, and trying to get my daughter to see that you just don't turn your back and walk away from family.

OK, and trying to get the hang of social media, and the husband to see my point when I'm trying to say something….

In light of this new reality, all of those challenges paled and seemed really petty.

Maybe it had always been a matter of perspectives?

Even now the pastor was saying something about having faith and trusting that God still has it all in control.

The pastor's wife was trying to get me to eat breakfast at noon. I decided at the last minute that the weight loss excuse would be a terrible one to use at this time, so I acquiesced to her imploring.

The husband looked like he knew without doubt that even this situation would work out for our good and to the glory of God — it must be because of all that time spent in the Word.

The friend was just ready to get this all done and over with. She'd reached out in the first place because she believed my daughter was out of her depths this time, and we were the only ones she could reach out to for help.

As they headed out the door, I prayed that God would help us. It wasn't a fancy prayer. It wasn't laced with theology, but it was heartfelt, and I had the assurance that He would help us.

Just when the peace that came after the prayer began to settle, the granddaughter woke from her nap.

The shrieking began.... And just like that, it felt like we were back where we were before the prayer.

I might be needing that aspirin now....

✳✳✳✳

I saw a meme one time that asked why we can't all just read good books and love each other.

Yes—

Why can't we?

Because then we wouldn't be hunting a daughter who's probably running for her life.

It turned out the couple my daughter didn't trust were detectives who were undercover. They'd gotten wind of what was going on at the children's home and were carrying out an investigation.

What we learned from the police would make anyone still with a conscience sick to the stomach.

For money, the children's home was giving out these children to literally anyone.

All they had to do was follow the already mapped out framework with background checks and all, but they had fallen on hard times and in a desperate attempt to not go bankrupt and fold, they were closing their eyes and disregarding red flags.

From the police, we learned that some of these children had been taken out of the country illegally and made to provide cheap labour. Others had ended up in the hands of people who sold them for their parts….

The story just went on, and it was horrifying.

They couldn't tell us everything as it was an ongoing investigation, but it just really surprised me, the depths the human heart could sink to if we let it.

In the meantime, they had made their presence visible at the home — thanks to my daughter, with the child theft and all! Word had gotten out and the ruckus it raised was no mean one.

And even though they were glad the screaming banshee was OK, we couldn't keep her. It was one of the hardest days of my life, watching them take from us, this child that had become part of our lives and family.

I've never felt as helpless as I did when she began to scream and reach for me, and there was nothing I could do to help.

News outlets and even blogs carried different versions of the story. Sometimes it was hard to know what they were talking about — you'd think they'd make the effort to get the story right before making it seem like they know what they're talking about.

It was hard to follow as my daughter was vilified in most of the reports. She was portrayed as a lowlife that should be made to pay for stealing a child and trying to set an orphanage on fire. *What?!*

The weeks this whole ordeal lasted were not the easiest ones. Sometimes it seemed like it would never end.

The husband kept saying we're Ok.

The pastor and his wife, and our church family too, kept checking in to see that we were Ok.

Friends visited us and offered to pray for us. They brought food and helped with the grandson. They cleaned the house and tried to do whatever they could to help.

The whole situation had left me unable to function properly, and the husband needed all the help I was unable to give at that time.

Just when I thought I couldn't deal with the situation anymore, we got a call that we were needed at the police station.

Again, the husband wouldn't let me go with him. He would go with the pastor — and they had the pastor's wife come over to be with me while they were gone.

I should be getting used to this by now, but it still didn't make it any easier. Waiting doesn't seem to be one of my strongest points, especially in circumstances like this present one!

But I couldn't do much to help — apart from praying, and hoping everything was still in God's control, that is.

The pastor's wife said it was more than enough, and she would join me.

So while we waited, we prayed and hoped that everything was still under God's control.

And we did our best to stay away from TV and social media.

The stories were assuming alarming dimensions….

And the situation was nothing aspirin could help with.

Sometimes, all the anxiety we have to deal with is as a result of not having a full knowledge of what we believe we know. Knowing in parts might not always be a good thing, because then we act on what is incomplete, and may never reach wholeness, except by a miracle from God. I learned this lesson again.

This whole while, I'd been in a perpetual state of anxiety, unable to function properly, and filed with a sense of foreboding, only to discover the situation had in fact always been under control.

Sometimes I think the husband always knew. Either that, or he just had this peace that could only have come from God.

Or he just knew very well, how to mask what he was feeling....

Because at no time, throughout this whole ordeal, did he seem as affected as I was — like, I was coming apart at the seams — literally.

At other times I think it's because of all that time he spends in the Word.

God's Word gives peace — perfect peace that passes understanding, no matter the circumstances or situations we find ourselves in. I learned this lesson again too.

So after this whole while, we find out our daughter was a detective working on this case, and it had been ongoing for a while.

The children's home had been on their radar long enough, they believed they had a case, so they had sent agents there.

I have no idea of the workings of that system, but everything they did was part of a plan.

Even the friend was playing a role (well… so much for all that sweetness as a child)!

They wouldn't tell us what they had found out because the investigation was still ongoing, but some powerful people would have to answer some questions. And the matron had to go!

And my daughter didn't turn her back on family!

After these many years, we find out it was all in a bid to protect us, as she worked dangerous cases with people that might be bent on seeking revenge as the arm of the law caught up with them.

She'd heard terrible stories of whole families being wiped out, and she was married to a detective who had lost friends because they were friends with detectives who went after people trying to run from the law.

And she didn't think she could be too careful — we didn't even know she worked with the police! We'd always thought she worked with computers.

All those years fretting, doubting and wondering, had it all been for nothing?

She had always been around, only not seen.

I wish she would have just said something from the beginning.

If I didn't know better, I could have sworn the husband had been saying the whole time after the discovery, "I told you so".

So now that we've learned lessons again, and discovered more of what we didn't know, I asked my daughter to adopt the shrieking banshee.

I may, or may not have blackmailed her, but I did mention that if she didn't, I would, and then the shrieking banshee would be her sister instead of her daughter.

It was a day of joy when she brought my now legit brand new granddaughter home. Even the grandson no longer seemed as fearful.

God was indeed working miracles.

And then from nowhere, amidst of all that joy, she said she was going on vacation to Paris with her husband. Really, this time.

I was so shocked, I spilled hot sauce on my hands!

As I tried to deal with the burn, the friend walked in carrying suitcases.

All I could do was pray, since it was almost impossible to process what was happening at this time — and it wasn't helping that the husband looked thoroughly amused and entertained.

These were desperate times! Dear Lord, help me! Do not let me live through that ordeal again! Please!

As the husband walked her to the car, while I tried to contain the drama the grandchildren were already creating, I overheard her ask about the weight loss program and the little black dress.

When she said, "It's been four years", I could almost hear the wheels spinning in my head.

I didn't tell her about that program or the dress in my wardrobe. And I definitely didn't tell her it's been four years.

Apart from me and the husband, no one else knew, and she wouldn't have that information unless one of us had told her.

It absolutely wasn't me, and it begged the question—
Had he been in touch with her the whole time?
Dear Lord, help me, please!
I should call the pastor's wife…. And get the bottle of aspirin….

7

Taking Things Out of the Basket

When you do a social media post, you do not expect your boss to read it. But that's what happened to me.

I wrote a post, my boss read it and fired me.

It was just a rant stemming from severe sleep deprivation and perplexity at how exhausted tiny humans can leave you.

I tried to explain. I didn't really mean what I'd written about how hard it was to go back to work mere months after birthing a child. I might have also said I hated my job (I deleted the post while pleading for my job, so I can't confirm this, but still…).

As if collecting evidence in a criminal case or something like that, she had screen grabbed the post — the whole thing! Can I just say how uncalled for and petty that was!

But I did say some things about the job. I'm not really sorry because I wasn't lying, I just didn't foresee this outcome. Now I have to live with the consequence of my decision to rant in a sleep-deprived, perplexed state.

I'd thought the most difficult part would have been coming home to a husband who had warned me countless times about my mouth.

"Think before you speak", he would say.

"I think before I speak", I always argue back.

After that one time I told the pastor's wife that she talked too much during women's meetings, we came up with a plan to wait a while before saying what comes to my mind.

It didn't take too long to realise we needed another plan.

It's not like I don't see his point about putting a filter over my words, it's just really hard to do sometimes. Add a newborn who keeps you up all day, every day to the mix and you'd be needing a miracle….

Like we do right now.

∗∗∗∗

Even with both of us working, we were barely able to keep our heads above water. Now it was nearly impossible.

He worked endless hours, while I sent out job applications and tried to start an online business.

We had this plan on paper that turned out completely different in real life, mostly because babies need a lot of things and these things cost a lot of money (Ok, maybe not really, but we're blaming the baby this time).

Time passed, and still, nothing turned out like we planned.

And I got tired of filling out applications.

I tried every business I heard I could do from home, but for some reason, nothing ever happened for me like the advertisements promised.

And sleep was still elusive.

After endless visits and doing my best to help him see my plight, the doctor finally recommended some pills to help me sleep. I was supposed to take them only as prescribed.

"Do you understand me?" he had asked, probably because I'd been as excited as a child in a candy shop. I know it doesn't sound right to be excited about something like that, but I'd heard all these things about how helpful these pills could be.

When I nodded, trying but failing woefully at hiding my excitement, he added, "You abuse these, and we'd stop".

"Yes sir", I said, taking the prescription. I left his office looking forward to at least seven hours of sleep.

It would be the first time in a long time, and it wasn't because of the baby. I just could no longer sleep and we didn't know why.

We tried everything....

Drink warm milk.

Count numbers.

Read books.

Listen to audiobooks.

Pray.

Read the Bible.

Essential oils....

Again, nothing had worked for me like the advertisements had promised.

✳✳✳✳

Just because you know something is wrong doesn't mean you won't do it.

And just because you know it won't do you any good doesn't mean you still won't do it.

This must be the meaning of addiction.

The sleeping pills worked, and before long, I was taking more than what was recommended — because... new baby, bills that grew without any corresponding increase in money available, no job, and a mind that chose to figure things out at night.

And a husband that profoundly disapproved of what he called abuse and misuse of prescription drugs.

118

I did not voluntarily push the self-destruct button on my life.

But I did push a button and began to spiral downwards to nothingness.

I only wanted to sleep.

At first, it was as easy as taking one or two more than was prescribed. Then they were finishing weeks before they were supposed to, and it became harder to keep up with the stories of why the bottles were getting empty so fast.

Soon there were these spells of dizziness, drowsiness, and weakness. I'm not sure what the pills were doing, but I was sick most of the time. And it was getting more difficult to pay attention and remember things.

The doctor wasn't too pleased that I'd disregarded his instruction to begin weaning myself off the pills. I told him I needed to sleep, but he said it wasn't necessary to exceed what was recommended. "You might have difficulty breathing. Or problems with your eyes. You might even start sleepwalking". I didn't believe him, so I stopped going to see him.

Eventually, I built a tolerance to them and needed more and more….

OK so I did find out my doctor knew what he was talking about, but by then just the thought of running out of the pills was enough to make me so anxious, I'd begin to hyperventilate.

And then I was told the problem was addiction.

To sleeping pills?

****

I had pushed the self-destruct button and I just kept spiraling downwards into nothingness in a black hole, all the while hoping that God would look on me with pity and help me.

I knew this addiction was wrong and wouldn't do me any good, yet I still indulged it.

But I did all I could.

All the self-help books I found led me in different directions, leaving me more perplexed as to why nothing seemed to be helping.

Then at church, the preacher said in times when it's hard to know what to do about situations we find ourselves in, we need to go to God's Word.

So I read it and listened to it, but nothing changed. At least it didn't seem like it to me.

I did the personal retreat.

Fasted.

And prayed all the prayers I knew how.

Nothing helped....

120

Eventually, I decided something was wrong because you don't encounter the Word of God and stay the same.

You don't meet with God in a personal retreat and stay the same.

And you certainly don't talk to the Father and stay the same.

Something was wrong, somewhere….

****

You know how sometimes God meets you in the middle of minding your own business? Like Moses, out with the flock, just like every other day, and then he sees a burning bush — except, the bush wasn't burning.

It happened to me….

I'd been at the store minding my own business when I happened upon a scene that refused to leave my mind.

A mother was at the store with her child. As they walked the aisles, the mother put things in their basket that the child took out. And the child put things in the basket that the mother took out. This went on for a while and stalled whatever progress might have been made.

The scene stuck with me, much to my chagrin, as it was none of my business. That night as I reached for the pills, it was as though I was that child at the store. I thought I was losing my mind when I heard the question, *"Don't you think the Father doesn't want that in the basket?"*

I ignored the question.

"Do you really need those?" I heard it again, *"What if the Father doesn't want that in the basket?"*

I needed to sleep, so I took what I needed and went to sleep.

But the question stayed with me. And the scene too….

What if the Father doesn't want that in the basket?

It took a while, but I finally began to ponder the question. I tried to remember how my dependence on these pills began. How did it get in the basket in the first place? And what's keeping it there?

What if the Father doesn't want it in the basket?

But He knows….

He knows how hard it is to get any sleep without them.

He knows how hard it is for my sleep-deprived self to get anything done.

It's not that easy to describe, but it's like a deep dark hole you can't get out of….

And it was absolutely not helping that from outside, my life looked put together, with not a single thing out of place. Everyone else seemed to believe I'm blessed, highly favoured, and without very much to worry about.

Maybe, but Lord knows the countless nights I was awake quoting Scriptures and claiming promises, still, worry and fear wouldn't leave.

I always wondered what I'd do if this constant state of apprehensiveness was my new reality.

Sometimes I wondered if it was only a matter of skewed perspectives, but then again, it wasn't that long ago I was getting a prescription. And then I was exceeding it.

And then time just went by until I was spiraling downward into that black hole of nothingness.

It was almost a free-fall.

✳✳✳✳

Every now and then, we happen upon a moment of grace that changes the course of our lives. You almost never see these moments coming, but then again, what is the definition of grace?

For me, it came with six words—

"You forgot to lock your door", an elderly man standing by my car told me. He was holding my baby.

After the incident with the mother and daughter at the store, there had been what I'd thought was an improvement. I'd finally agreed with the doctor that it was time to stop taking the pills, and we'd been working to wean me off them.

123

Everything was going as planned until one morning when it wasn't.

I'd woken up feeling very out of sorts, and for no particular reason that I could think of.

My restlessness only grew worse as the day progressed. By noon, I decided my problem was sleep. I'd slept through the night, but I still reckoned that was the problem. I don't even know why.

I have a challenge with my mouth, and a husband that's well acquainted with this challenge. After that one time I called him at work, ranting and raving about his boss, we decided it was best to text rather than call him at work. Even I could see why it was better this way. He'd been in a meeting with said boss. But I couldn't text today because my hands were trembling.

And I wasn't going to call the doctor. I was just going to go and get those pills.

As there was no one else around, I went with the baby.

The weather wasn't hot but I was sweating profusely and my trembling hands made me wonder just a little bit, how safe it was to drive to the store in my current state, with a baby in the back seat.

I was just going to dash in and out of the store — it usually didn't take that long — and then we'd go straight back home.

And that's what happened. I dashed in and out of the store.

And then I came out and saw a man standing by my car, holding a baby.

It did not immediately seem like something to be concerned about until I got closer and realised he was holding my baby.

Many thoughts raced through my mind so fast, it was hard to zero in on any one and decide on a course of action.

I brought my phone out and put it back in my purse.

I started to run, but realised I would have spent whatever energy was still available to me, by the time I got to the car.

Finally, I sent a cry for help to heaven.

By the time I got to the car, I was still concerned, but not afraid.

And then, that moment of grace that came with those six words....

****

In my haste, I'd left the door on the driver's side unlocked. This kind gentleman had noticed it. He had been passing by and had first been drawn by the baby's crying.

What if…?

I needed to take things out of the basket because—

What if…?

The preacher says it's not enough to hear the Word just for hearing sake. You need to hear it with faith, and then you need to be obedient and do what you've heard.

It's not enough to fast, pray and have a retreat. You need to do it with faith, expecting to find God as you seek Him, and then you need to listen, follow Him, and be obedient and do what He says.

We read in the Bible that without faith we cannot please God or even come to Him.

And that was exactly what I needed, to get out of that hole — what I heard, and what I did, I needed to do with faith.

As I threw the pills out, there was that anxiety and hyperventilating, but I was ready to get out of that dark hole.

I was taking this out of the basket.

And everything else I cannot do with faith.

8

And…the Plan Is STILL Up in the Air

There was blood, shards of broken glass, and plastic everywhere. The altar boy had just karate chopped his sister's hand, sending her phone flying. Worshippers, reacting by reflex, pushed the missile forward with flailing arms and considerable force until it landed on the head of a dozing worshipper.

It was during the first prayer session.

With eyes wide as saucers, his mother looked ready to disappear from where she sat watching the commotion her son had begun. And then as if awakened from a vision, she hurried out of her seat, reached the offending child, and dragged him out of the sanctuary by the ear for the second time that day.

She had dragged him down that same aisle by the ear earlier before the worship service had begun, after she caught him playing outside with other boys from children's church. He was supposed to be with the preacher getting ready for the service but he had been with these boys who were supposed to be using the bathroom. Before long their teachers were swarming the place, trying to get them back as quietly as they could — something that was never an easy task to accomplish.

It was always the same. Sunday after Sunday after Sunday....

The front of his shirt was wet from her efforts to restore the shirt as close as she could, to the state it had been in when they got to church, and she was chiding him for getting his shirt dirty with stains impossible to remove.

His sister did her best to keep her composure and not add to the unfolding drama, but she was a sorry sight as she all at once tried to salvage what was left of her broken phone, apologise to the worshipper who had been hit on the head, and also reassure fellow worshippers that her bleeding face was just surface wound.

✳✳✳✳

They say no one really has life figured out.

Not this mother.

She always knew exactly where she was going, and how to get there. And she had covered enough ground to bolster faith and generate sufficient momentum to keep her going and reinforce her belief that no plans or goals were too impossibly out of reach.

She had faced life with a certain confidence based on this belief that no problems were unsolvable.

Detours were adventures she wasn't afraid to explore — because, everything eventually resolves itself.

But that was all before children.

You know how they always say children change the dynamics and test your convictions? She didn't believe them.

Her path was set. The map was sure. She would train her children and lead them in the way they should go.

Now she sympathises with every woman with a new child.

"It's not like it's not a good thing…. Children are a blessing… because that's what it says in the Bible…. But your life has been changed, and you don't even know how much".

Just look at me now.

Now she believes life took that *no-problems-are-unsolvable* notion and decided to teach her a lesson on that view.

Because—

"Look at me now". It has become the meaning, and the answer to whatever life chooses to send her way.

It didn't matter what the situation was, at some point — eventually — the conclusion was "Look at me now".

And it always made sense.

Take the altar boy for instance….

Even though he's still only just a child, everyone is terrified of him.

It's true. That's how come he even began to help at the altar, in the first place.

They tried everything at children's church.

They had him sit in a corner and memorise the books of the Bible, and the names of the twelve sons of Jacob, and the names of the twelve disciples, and the names of the churches in Revelations.

(All this, while they did normal children's church activities with the other children).

Everyone feels sorry for him, but he can't go back to children's church because then all the teachers would start calling in sick (well, almost all of them).

And you can't blame them.

The words that came out of his mouth as questions (Every. Single. Time.) are a terror to the ears of the ordinary Sunday school teacher who didn't go to seminary yet.

And he's still only just a child.

So they brought him to main church, and he became the altar boy.

All he had to do was help the preacher. Basically, just do whatever he was told to do, like carry trays during communion, or help the preacher carry his Bible sometimes, or pass messages to conductors during worship services.

Easy — except he kept falling asleep on his knees every time, and complaining that the prayers were too long. It wasn't that easy for him to sit still when the preacher was giving the message. And he always got hungry, and would tell his mother so in a loud whisper, much to her dismay.

 His sister wouldn't stop recording the whole thing — he on his knees, falling asleep, and suddenly jerking awake (probably from the chilling glare his mother aimed his way — like, if looks could kill! Seriously!) It's hard to know what she plans to do with all the recordings, because it's usually the same thing every Sunday (well, almost every Sunday, except for the ones like today when it goes a bit farther and he does something extra like hitting the head of a dozing worshipper with a phone).

✳✳✳✳

"I didn't even want to come", her son told her as she dragged him down the aisle.

She ignored him and told his sister to go to children's church. The teachers had come to get the wayward boys.

When she saw her daughter's bleeding face, she almost came undone. She alternated between tending the wound and shaking her son, while telling him how much trouble he had caused at church that morning.

He told her if she continued to shake him like that she would give him a headache.

A lot of worshippers had opinions on how best to handle the situation and most gave them.

"Just let him be…. He's just a child and he would outgrow this phase".

"You need to train him now before this behaviour gets out of hand".

"He needs prayers. A lot of it".

"This is why a boy needs his father".

The array of opinions was confusing and annoying.

What exactly were they telling her to do?

She stood at the entrance of the sanctuary for a while. Her son was talking, but it was clear he wasn't reaching her.

She stood there, looking at her children — almost like a valuer trying to determine their worth.

When her son asked if they could go home, kind worshippers took him away before she could get to him.

"I didn't even want to come", he kept saying.

Other worshippers tried to reassure her.

When those with the array of opinions began to give them again, she bit her tongue to try to keep the situation from getting out of hand.

Maybe they really did mean to help (some of them, at least), but at that moment, not only were their words confusing and annoying, they were also like salt on open wound.

She would go home and tend the wound — sulk a bit maybe, mourn the loss of the path she had given up, and then she would get back up and continue in this present path.

She would count her blessings and continue to be a mother. Like a jeweller, she would keep cutting and polishing, hoping that the day would finally come when she would see a reward for all that work.

And she would try church again.... Maybe next week.

But today, she got her things and her children, and left for home.